The Cougar Contract

Victoria Sanford

The Cougar Contract

Published in the United States of America
341 Enterprise
Copyright 2021 by Victoria Sanford
ISBN: 978-1-7353435-9-4

This is a work of fiction. Except for historical and famous characters, all characters, names, places, and events appearing in this work are a product of the author's imagination or used fictitiously. Any resemblance to real persons, living or dead, is entirely coincidental.

Dedicated To

Tiffiny Nicole Kilgore

My cougar-
who would fit right in with

the Pride.

Chapter 1

Gwen Marlow wasn't sure which one she hated more, hospital or airport waiting rooms. Both areas made her a nervous wreck. Her eyes went to the clock on the wall, the old fashioned clock that said they should have been in the air twenty minutes ago. She was tired of flipping through pages of out of date fashion magazines filled with clothes she would never wear, even if she could afford them. Outside, the rosy glow of the sun was peeking over the eastern horizon. She had arrived before the flight was scheduled to leave, ready to get this trip over with and get back to her normal life. Instead, she had been sitting for two hours, staring out the window at the small commuter plane sitting on the runway outside the combination hanger and reception area. Waiting on the missing pilot to appear.

The freckle faced teenager behind the reception desk lay down her cell phone for the first time in over an hour and said something to her mother, an older version with the same brassy red hair, except the older woman's hair was liberally streaked with shades of grey. Then she called out, "Coffee's ready. Would you like a cup? Or would you prefer a coke?"

"Coffee is fine. Thanks, cream, no sugar." A faintly cynical grimace turned her tight lips into a softer, more sensual smile that hinted at multiple underlying layers of personality.

The girl vanished through a set of swinging doors, then returned in moments carrying two ceramic cups, both filled with steamy hot liquid.

"Tired of waiting," she asked as she passed the cup to Gwen.

"Long past tired," she replied. "Any idea when he will arrive?"

"Tyrel is usually right on time. As far back as I can remember this is the first time he has even been late. There has to be a good reason for the delay, even though it may not seem like it was right to you."

Gwen sighed. Nothing about this trip seemed like a good decision. The visit was not her idea. Her father had contacted her and insisted she come and stay for her eighteenth birthday. He had purchased the ticket to fly her from Fort Smith to Atlanta and chartered the private plane to take her on the final leg of her journey into the Smokey Mountains. Her green and topaz eyes darkened, and she flipped her long auburn hair impatiently. She had no interest in meeting her father's side of the family or her half-siblings. Her parents had divorced when she was six. Over the years her father had visited her twice a year, on her birthday and at Christmas. At first, she had looked forward to his visits, but over the years the importance of a visit by a man she only saw occasionally became less of a treat and more of a disruption to her life.

The extended wait in the tiny airport hangar was hardly conducive to relieving the stress she was experiencing. No one else seemed to be upset about the pilots' tardiness.

The swinging door between the reception and the hangar opened and a man stuck his head out, "Ty just called. He's fifteen minutes out."

"Gotcha," the girl called back before walking through the interior door.

The older man stepped into the room, a big, welcoming grin on his face. "Let me grab your bags and get them stowed away."

Gwen released the breath she hadn't been aware she was holding and relaxed. Fifteen more minutes. She pasted a fake smile on her face and tried to remain calm. There had to be a good reason for the delay. She pointed at her feet. "There's just the two."

"Your folks from around Transylvania?" He picked up the bags, ready to take them out to the plane.

"Somewhere near there. We are going to a private landing field in the area. Someone I'm related to runs it. I'm not sure exactly where it is. Near Lake

Toxaway. But your pilot is supposed to be familiar with the area."

He nodded. "Ty grew up near there. If anyone knows the area, he does. You could not ask for a better pilot. If he would just get here… Damn, she was pretty when she smiled. He would take the girl himself if he were forty years younger. The twinkles in his eyes were the only hints of what he was thinking. "Ty is a bit of a lone wolf, but one hell of a pilot. He knows the mountain terrain better than anyone."

Gwen wondered why he was not loading her cases into the airplane. Even that small thing would make her feel like they were getting somewhere. Instead, he stood in the doorway, looking off into the eastern sky.

"Finally," he mumbled under his breath as the approaching helicopter seemed to appear out of the sun itself. He watched the tiny dot grow bigger as it neared the airport. As the helicopter was landing, he picked up her bags. That's when Gwen realized she would be traveling in the copter, not the small jet setting on the tarmac. This was a pleasant surprise. She had always wanted to fly in a helicopter, but the opportunity had never come up. It was another check off her bucket list. The past year had brought about a lot of firsts in her life. She had recently completed her first year at the local community college, broken up with her high school boyfriend, and moved into a small efficiency apartment in the complex her mother owned. It wasn't much on the grand scheme of things but after being sheltered most of her like, it felt great to be on her own.

As the helicopter settled on the ground, she got her first look at the man who would be flying her to see her father. She had built a preconceived image of the pilot in her mind, imagining a short, sickly, middle-aged man with a beer belly and a receding hairline. The man sliding out of the pilots' seat was nothing like this. For one thing, he was tall, well over six feet, and what her mother would have called a fox. He wore a blue flannel button-up open over a black HAIM t-shirt that stretched tightly over his muscular chest. She let a brief smile break her neutral expression. The pilot's choice in T's provided a welcome change after thousands of Post Malone and Chain Smoker t-shirts worn by pudgy first-year students at her school. The blue flannel shirt he wore did nothing to disguise the array of muscles that flexed in his broad shoulders as he reached for her bags and placed them in the space behind his seat. He wore his onyx colored hair long, pulled back into a thick horsetail that reached the middle of his back. A few stray curls framed his face, drawing attention to his amazingly long black eyelashes. Eyes the color of spring honey flecked with green sparkled boldly. The hazel color drew attention to the prominent cheekbones and strong jawline on a weathered bronze face that would have been at home on any romance book cover. The golden undertones of his ruddy skin held a hint of Asian blood but it was clear he was at least half Native American. It seemed almost criminal to find all that in one man.

He was much younger than Gwen expected him to be, most likely in his mid-twenties, but he somehow gave off the impression he was much older...in control at all times. She liked that he was cleanly shaven, but the first hints of a five o'clock shadow were already peeping through. He stood at the door expectantly, the slightest smirk on his lips and the kind of eyes you could drown in.

She rose to her feet, expecting some kind of apology for being so late.

His stern gaze acknowledged her presence, noted her jeans and tee-shirt, and her bright red high heels, and cataloged her assets then immediately turned his attention back to the old man Howard. "Hate to ask, but would you top me off while I hit the head and grab a sandwich? My last trip took longer than I expected. No time for breakfast."

When Howard nodded and walked out the door he disappeared into the hanger without a word to Gwen.

Arrogant bastard. Gwen fought back the impulse to turn and walk back to the main terminal. It would be so simple to catch the next flight back to Fort Smith. It was his fault they were running behind not hers.

He had a donut in his hand when he returned. "Ready to go?"

Gwen's fingers tightened on her purse. He had the nerve to ask her if she was ready! As if she had been the one almost an hour late. The sound of her heels clicking on the asphalt was loud as she struggled to match his long stride. As he veered toward the driver's side, she started toward the passenger side of the helicopter. Since there was only one available seat, it was obvious where she would be sitting. It took her three tries to get inside, but she finally climbed in beside him. After wedging her purse in beside the seat, Gwen sunk into the soft leather seat. Once she was comfortable, she fastened her seat belt and stared out the window at the busy airport. It was going to be a long flight.

***

Ty hid the twitch of his lips as his passenger attempted to climb into the waiting helicopter. Normally he would have offered to help, but he had realized that any offer of assistance he made, would be taken as a challenge by the spitfire seated beside him. He wondered why she was heading toward the mountain. And why Gideon had asked him to pick her up.

"Let's get this bird off the ground." At the push of a button, the helicopter's engines roared to life, the oversized propeller hesitating for a second, then spinning faster and faster until little more than a blur.

When she thought he wasn't looking, she glanced at her sweaty palms, then wiped them on her handkerchief. As the helicopter blades began to spin faster, he could see her body tighten up.

"Don't be nervous, I've been flying for years." Tyrel liked how the feisty woman smiled at him with soft eyes when he looked down at her, even though the smile only lasted a few seconds. Besides his mother, she was the first woman that carried a handkerchief he'd seen. It was old fashioned but kinda cute.

His passenger had settled back in her seat and was silently staring out the window as the helicopter accelerated before lifting off from the ground.

The noise of the engine while sitting on the ground made conversation impossible, so Tyrel gestured for her to put on the headphones clipped to the dash panel and eased back on the control, sending the chopper upward. Once he reached the height he wanted he pushed the lever forward and began heading toward their destination.

Ty cast a sideways glance at her left hand, noting there was no ring on her finger. So she wasn't engaged. Strangers were uncommon in the area of North

Carolina she was heading to. Especially around the mountain. She was looking out the glass at the landscape as they t/7raveled north toward the state line. It was going to take about an hour to reach North Carolina and then another half hour to reach her destination. They would have to fly slower once they reached the mountains because of the terrain. He wished he had paid more attention to Aggie when she reserved the flight. Gwen… that much he remembered. He had been watching the race and his driver had just spun out, putting him a lap down on the pack. Her last name had gone right past him. It was printed on the manifest in his jacket pocket, but that was lying in the back underneath her two bags. The only way he would get answers was to ask. What the Hell.

"So,.. your father is from Wolf Mountain?"

"I assume so." Her father had taken care of the travel details and she hadn't cared enough to study where she was going. At this point-in-time, she wasn't even sure why she was going. It had happened so fast. She had just returned home from school when the phone rang. The invitation had been unexpected, after so many years she had not expected to hear from him at all. "I don't even know if my father is going to meet me at the airport. I wasn't able to talk to him before I left the house this morning. But since he made the arrangements with you himself, I'm sure he told you where to drop me."

Ty was surprised by her answer. Gideon was her father? Wow. Talk about being slapped in the face. This was a major detail to forget to mention. "How long has it been since you've seen him?"

"About three years...he had some things he needed to work out before I could visit."

Boy was that an understatement.

"Are you familiar with the area?" she asked.

Tyrel nodded, "My great-great-grandparents bought land on the mountain close to 200 years ago. The farm has been passed down through the generations. I hope you'll forgive me for not immediately recognizing you."

Gwen exhaled, "To be honest, I would have been surprised if you had."

"Most everyone in the area is related in some way." He smiled. "You take after your mother. I imagine being the daughter of a famous movie star can be a bit overwhelming."

She nodded. "It can be trying." If she was being truthful, saying it was overwhelming, was an understatement. Nothing could explain the insanity that came with having a famous mother. Between the sycophantic fans, the total lack of privacy in public, and the other stars, she had never been happy on a film site. She was Sophia's daughter first, not

Gwendolyn, losing even the limited sense of identity that all teenagers enjoyed.

The only thing she could depend on was her father When her mother took a big role, everything in her life changed, except for him. When she was young she had to pick up and move to wherever the movie was filming. Leaving any friends she had managed to make behind had often devasted her confidence. She eventually gave up trying to bond with anyone, becoming withdrawn and silent instead. Then her father would show up and make life livable again.

By the time she finally old enough to understand who her mother was, the damage had already been done. Her father had disappeared, and with him went any chance of normalcy. Several psychiatrists had tried to help her, but she had come to hate everything about society, the movie business, and life in the city.

She began staying at home when her mother traveled for a film. Not that anyone forgot who her mother was, they simply changed tactics. As she got older the paparazzi and journalists had begun using a different approach, trying to wiggle their way into her life using everything from flattery to outright lies. One had even pretended to go to her school and asked her out on a date as an excuse to talk to her mother.

The small college in Arkansas was perfect. No one knew her mother. Once she was ensconced in her room at the college she had been happy to escape into anonymity.

"I was hoping to keep my presence a secret. I rarely get the opportunity to enjoy a vacation."

Laugh lines creased Tyrel's mouth. "Well, unfortunately, that won't be an option. No one on the mountain can keep a secret, and Gideon likes to gossip with the rest of the residents. Everybody will know who you are from the moment you arrive."

This was disappointing. She doubted her father had many photos of me and the ones he had were old. She had been looking forward to being nothing more than Gideons daughter.

Tyrel watched the disappointment cross her features and wished he had never mentioned that he knew who she was. For some reason, he felt an odd urge to protect her. Maybe it was because she was Gideon's daughter?

The air from his AC vent ruffled the edge of her hair, and she automatically shoved it behind her ear. He grinned, thinking it was a shame she was so uncomfortable. The early morning sun coming through the windshield brought out the red in her auburn hair, making it appear as if flickering flames surrounded her face. None of her features were what he considered classically beautiful, but they combined in a surprisingly attractive package. Ty found himself intrigued. He had a million questions he wanted to ask her but many of them would make him sound insane, so he kept his mouth shut and his eyes on the terrain instead of the girl.

Why was she going to the mountain?

Chapter 2

The tiny rural airport was dark when they landed but Tyrel did not seem surprised. They had embedded reflectors into the concrete landing pad making it easy to locate the designated area from the air. As the blades of the helicopter slowed to a stop, Gwen was out of her seatbelt and walking toward the building before the handsome young pilot announced it was safe to do so.

Noticing where she was headed, Ty pointed to a vintage Ford pickup sitting beside the main building. "That's my truck. It's unlocked. Hop in while I grab your bags."

She immediately changed the direction she was walking and did as he asked. He watched as she walked directly to the truck, opened the door, and slid inside.

He was surprised when she didn't comment about the age of the truck. Most women tend to judge you by the amount of money you spend on a vehicle. The truck had belonged to his grandfather and meant more to him than any new off the lot pickup ever could. Other than dusting off the old patchwork quilt he left over the seat, she didn't appear the least bit put out about the transportation. She even accepted him placing the expensive leather bags in the bed of the truck without comment. Tyrel mentally adjusted his opinion of her upward. It was rare he met someone coming from her background without the overblown ego associated with it.

"That's the town?" Gwen asked as she looked down at the road through the narrow valley. Situated along the road were a small post office, a slightly bigger country store, and about a dozen framed wood houses. It turned out to be a smaller city than she'd expected. They had traveled to the area on the Smokey Mountain Parkway in their rush to reach her father's cabin before noon. She spotted an old-fashioned Gas station called Cody's that looked like it came out of a vintage Mayberry segment, and grinned as Ty pulled in. The old man in the rocker could have walked right off the show. He was wearing overalls that were at least two sizes too big, a white tee-shirt, and a striped cap with the gas station's name embroidered above the bill. He spat a chaw of tobacco into a battered brass spittoon at his feet and shambled over to pump her gas. While the tank filled, he washed the windshield and checked the oil. Gwen had heard about full-service stations, but this was the first one she'd actually seen.

The old man looked from Gwen in the passenger seat to the man standing by the counter then back to Gwen. "That who I think it is?"

"Most likely."

Cody didn't ask a lot of questions but Ty could see the curiosity reflected in his eyes.

"I need to go pay for the gas. You can get out and stretch your legs if you like, there's a pond beside the building. It's going to take a few minutes."

"Is it okay if I go inside," she asked.

"Yes, go ahead. Edith keeps a wide variety of things inside. You may see something you want."

"Thank you, I would like that." She stretched, arching her back like a house cat with a contented sigh.

Tyrel noticed that she had to stop and slide her feet back into her shoes. She pulled her cellphone out to check her messages, then frowned when she realized there were no bars.

"Tyrel?

He spun around. "Yes?"

"I can't get a signal on my phone."

"Might as well leave all of your electronic stuff in your bag. There's been no signal since we turned off the bypass."

"None at the cabin?" Her voice rose in pitch as the possibility of being completely cut off sink in.

"Nope. They might have a landline, but chances are they ride over to the ski lodge if they need to talk to someone."

"No internet?"

"Nope."

"Great," she said. "They do have indoor plumbing, right?"

He laughed at her attempt at sarcasm. "I'm sure they can accommodate you. Thirsty? I'll grab us something to drink."

"Thanks. Coke, please."

Tyrel's eyes followed her as she walked toward the building, enjoying the way she moved. Some women had to work at it but she was naturally sexy.

Once Cody finished topping off his tank, Tyrel moved the old black ford to a parking spot between two newer extended cab trucks, grabbed his wallet from the glove box, and followed her as she walked toward the country store's open screened door.

An older grey-haired woman with leathery skin leaned against the polished wooden counter. Her dark eyes tracked Gwen as she walked toward the sign saying bathrooms but made no comment. She was clearly curious but willing to wait and see how much info was offered.

Edith looked up as Tyrel came inside but went back to stacking cans. As he walked back to the

18

counter she gave him a friendly nod. "Two drinks? You got company with you?"

"Just dropping off a passenger." He opened a black ledger she laid on the counter and made a notation about his purchase, listing his gas and the drinks. He saw her eyes widen as she put two and two together.

"Well, I'll be damned. Gideon really does have a daughter. Otto is gonna be tickled pink. She's a right purty 'lil thing."

Otto. Ty had forgotten about him. Rumor was he had won the girls hand in a poker game. She must be here to complete the contract. For some odd reason, she felt the need to hide the fact. Most likely for the same reason she had tried to hide her blood. As if he couldn't smell her as soon she sat down in the copter beside him.

Tyrel was surprised she had not acknowledged him, but maybe she was intent on reaching her destination and assumed he know all about her. He remembered his aunt mentioning something about Gideon having a daughter before she had died; some sketchy outline about them marrying before his transition, a midlife separation, and a baby he had never planned on. He could believe it.

He had assumed she was older, but that meant his passenger was close to her eighteenth birthday. She had not transitioned, so she may not have recognized what he was. But she must be close, or he would not have able to identify her by her scent. Now he understood why Gideon had sent for her.

Tyrel had been in the Army when the change came on him the first time. He had locked himself in the bathroom at a bar, refusing to come out for over an hour as he fought to get his turbulent emotions under control. And he had been raised in the pack. He could imagine how his city born and bred passenger was going to take it, especially since her mother was human. Living by the rules of the Pride was going to be a big change.

Now that he thought about it, she seemed pretty calm for someone who was about to marry a total stranger. She couldn't be too excited to learn the person her father intended for her to marry was old enough to be her father.

Finally, curiosity got him and he carefully broached the subject. "I know it's not my business but has it been a while since you last saw your father?"

There was a slight pause before she answered. " Yes. About five years. He would drop by when he was in California but he changed jobs and the visits became less often. To be honest, I was surprised when he called and suggested I come and visit him for my birthday."

"Your birthday?"

"Yes. I will be eighteen the day after tomorrow." She chuckled. "I had to shift a lot of things around to make this trip. "I'm supposed to be in class today. It's going to be a pain catching up the days I miss but it won't be the first time I had to do extra work to keep up my studies."

"You're still in school?" This surprised him. He had thought she was slightly older, out of high school at least.

"My second year of college, University of Arkansas. I'm working on my engineering degree, Robotics, and Unmanned Aerial Systems. "

Now Ty was even more mystified. This wasn't some immature young girl who was going to meekly do what her father said. Not many made it to the second year of college before turning eighteen. And studying to be an Engineer. What the hell was Gideon thinking? "Does your father know any of this?"

Tyrel's question surprised her. Did her father know? She had no idea. It had not come up in the conversation. He had simply asked her to come to visit him. He had called back an hour later and mentioned he had left a plane ticket in her name at the airport terminal. They had not talked that long; it was more a case of him taking and her listening. He'd mentioned being sick. That day his voice was gravelly, making it hard to understand some of what he was saying. She had been more interested in getting him off the phone so she could go back to the movie she was watching than anything. Now she wondered what else she might have missed. She had only thought about seeing him and spending time with him in the Smokey's.

The mountains were gorgeous. As they drove along the parkway toward Wolf Mountain Community she had been surprised by how many birds there were in the area. Birds had been on her mind. Last night she had the strangest dream. What made it strange was that she was the only human in the dream, everyone else was an animal. There were also several hawks and a great horned owl. One of the hawks flew toward her and landed on the branch of the tree where she had hung a rabbit she had recently snared for her dinner. Then the owl lands and scares the hawk away. She had always been attracted to owls so she moved out of her hiding spot to get a closer look. As she walked around to the other side of the tree, she almost steps in the way of an enormous cougar trying to catch a hawk. The cougar pounces on the bird, and she ducked into a large hole in the tree to hide. But the big cat finds her. For some reason, she was not afraid. She decided to crawl past him out of the hole and go about her way. The cougar sniffs her on her way out and lets her pet him. As she stands up and walks away, the cougar walks with her, and stays by her side. She knew somehow he was meant to be with her.

Now, if the dream had been about wolves she could have understood it. She loved Twilight and all the associated books and movies. She had never been much of a cat person, but now that she thought about it, dogs didn't like her either. They either growled or slunk away as if they were afraid.

"Are there a lot of wild animals in the area?"

Ty shot her a puzzled look before he answered. "Yes. Quite a variety. The Smokey's are famous for wildlife. Everyone knows about the bears, but wolves and coyotes are running in packs, as well as the more reclusive bobcats and mountain lions. You might see deer and elk casually wandering through town. Not to mention all the smaller animals like porcupines, beavers, and squirrels."

"Seems like there are a lot of birds, too. That's a hawk, isn't it?"

"A Redtail. He's hunting, see how he flies back and forth across the field like he's following a grid? He will cover the entire area in his search."

She watched the hawk until they had moved too far away for her to see it anymore. She was surprised by how many dirt roads they passed between the small private airstrip and the next small community.

"Are there a lot of wolves near my father's house?" She had her nose pressed to the window like a little girl, watching the terrain as they passed. She spotted a trio of deer, but no wolves.

"I'm sure there are some in the forest but the Wolf the mountain was named after is a family. This was all Cherokee land at one time. In the late 1800s many were forced off their land when Gold was discovered in North Georgia. Over the years a lot of their descendants have moved back to the Qualla area and work in Cherokee. The Wolfs refused to give up their land, they built a ski resort on one side to have income and a town on the opposite side. The Wolf lands run from the lake back to the old state highway. Almost everyone living in this area is related. It's rare to even see visitors on this side of the mountain.

"So you are related to my father?" The pilot seemed alright. He was polite and knew everyone by name yet he talked as if he was an outsider. She wondered how he tied in with the residents. His answer surprised her.

"By marriage. At one time he was married to my aunt. She died in an accident two years ago. Many cousins still live in the area. In fact...," he pointed to a white frame house with a picket fence out front that was briefly visible through the trees, "...that's my mother's house. I will spend the night there and catch up before I get an early start back to Atlanta tomorrow."

"So you are a Wolf?"

"Among other things." He grinned, showing incredibly white teeth. His eyes twinkled merrily amidst the smallest hint of laugh lines.

Gwen had realized he was at least part Cherokee from his tawny skin color, but the gilded amber eyes must have come from his father. The afternoon sun made the greenish highlights in his eyes appear to glow. She was surprised by how attractive he was. She rarely met a man she could sit and talk to this way. So many men his age were sexually aggressive or assumed she was out to trap a husband and avoided a conversation.

"My mother was a Wolf. My Father was a Henderson. You could say I have a lot of him in me." His eyes seemed to darken, and she wondered what he was hiding.

Before she got a chance to ask another question, Ty turned off Highway 281 onto a winding country road that had a number instead of a name. Part of the road was in bad shape and looked like it hadn't been scraped or maintained in years. Until she was almost bounced out of the seat, Gwen hadn't given much thought to anything except the scenery. Unfortunately, no one had mentioned the horrible condition of the dirt road leading up the back side of the mountain. The sheer drop off looked closer than she was comfortable with. After several miles, she realized the pickup's four-wheel-drive setup was having no difficulty traveling along the rutted dirt roadway and relaxed.

Lately, finding peace was almost impossible. Her personal life had gone to pieces, but she had a good feeling about this trip. The doctors had not been optimistic about her mother's recovery after her stroke. There had been massive damage to her frontal lobe, enough that she needed around the clock care and help with everyday necessities, like dressing or baths. She got the best care Gwen could afford, but sometimes, even with her insurance it was difficult.

When she had stopped by the night before she left town to tell her mother she was leaving to visit her father, she had clung to her hand until she fell asleep. Gwen hated that her mother could no longer talk, it made it hard to communicate. She was certain her mother had been trying to tell her something important. She made a mental note to stop in and see her as soon as she got back home.

The Smokey Mountains brought her the same feeling of serenity that nights with her mother once had. Now that she was in the nursing home, it was harder to find that comfortable sweet spot she had grown to depend on. She hoped this trip would change that.

Her father used to call the Smokey Mountains 'Natures Wonderland', often quoting President Franklin D. Roosevelt who said, "There are trees here that stood before our forefathers ever came to this continent, there are brooks that still run as clear as on the day the first pioneer cupped his hand and drank from them."

She had never understood what he meant until today. It was beautiful here. It was early fall so the forest was heavily overgrown but she was sure it was just as beautiful when all the leaves were gone. I bet it's beautiful in the winter, once the snow covers everything in a white blanket. Fort Smith occasionally got a little snow but it never lasted. She was lucky if she managed to snap a few photos before the neighborhood kids turned it into grey slush. One day she hoped to experience the real deal, building a snowman, sliding on a sled, even a snowball fight. If I can find someone to fight with...

She sat back and looked out the window watching for the yellow mailbox. There were not a lot of homes along the road they were traveling down but her father had told her there was no way she could miss it.

She broke out laughing when she saw it. It was shaped like a duck and painted a brilliant yellow with a blue bow around its neck. The driveway itself was graveled and in good condition. She could see a couple of cows and a trio of horses in the paddock as they approached the house. The trees to either side were festooned with yellow ribbons that dance in the light breeze. Her father had never been a pet person, so the sight of the large black tuxedo cat lying on the porch railing surprised her.

Her father's cabin was in better shape than Tyrel had led her to expect. It wasn't enormous, but the rocking chair front porch made it seem bigger. Someone had hung a swing at one end of the porch and a nearby hammock was placed in the perfect spot to catch the cool Indian summer breeze.

There was electricity. The front porch light on, and they had nailed a bright yellow bow to the front door. This simple welcome drove all the uncertainties away from her mind. There were even signs of a woman in the cabin, frilly, light-colored curtains on the windows that indicated a feminine hand in the décor. This made her feel a bit better, she had never been alone with her father. He must have been watching for her arrival because the door opened as soon as they pulled in. He continued to stare at her as she got out of the truck and walked across the yard to the porch, then welcomed her with a warm smile and a hug.

"I was beginning to think you were not coming," he declared.

"Why would you think that. I was happy to hear from you after so long."

His face twisted for a few seconds before going back to the broad smile she associated with him. "I wasn't sure you could get away with your mother being in a nursing home."

"The only reason I could get away is that she is in a nursing home. I know she is being well taken care of and that they will contact me if anything changes."

"You look so grown," he said. "I am so happy to have you here with me." He wrapped her in his arms and squeezed, the same kind of loving bear hug he had always given her. She began to feel better.

A slight harrumph caught her attention and she turned to the stranger who had moved up to stand next to her father. He was a big, casually dressed, rough-looking man that instantly made her skin crawl. For one thing, he was looking at her like she was some type of meat, cut and displayed in a butcher's shop, that he was grading for fat content, taste, and texture. Her father's greeting was cut short as the strange man wrapped her in a rib-bruising hug. "You are even prettier than your father said you would be. I look forward to getting to know you. Your birthday is when, Saturday? That's perfect!"

Gwen wiggled out of the strangers' python-strong embrace wondering what was perfect about her birthday being Saturday. She glanced at her father but he was telling Tyrel to put her bags on the porch. Ty said something to him that made him flush and shift his weight uncomfortably. His face tightened the way it always did when he argued with her mother.

She turned to Otto. "I will be right back I think I left something in the truck." Then she rushed off the porch before he could answer. Opening the passenger door on Ty's truck, she reached into her shirt and pulled out a silver pendant she wore around her neck. It was engraved with the words Many things may catch your eye; pursue only those that capture your heart. She hooked the pendant around a mirror on his dashboard and walked back to the house. She had no idea why she did. It was not very large; it might be a while before he noticed it. It made her feel better leaving a subtle reminder that she was there. Her father was still talking to Tyrel when she returned to the porch.

Whatever they were talking about seemed to irritate Tyrel. His eyes went to her and he snapped out something to her father, something that made his skin pale. Instead of walking back over to her, Ty called out, "I'm taking off. Hope you enjoy your time here." He waved his hand over his head, got into his truck, and drove off.

Ty caught the look of fear in her eyes and had second thoughts about leaving her there. He felt bad about leaving her the way he did but there was nothing he could say to help her. Her father had signed the handfast contract when she was three. By their laws she was legally bound to marry Otto. The only way she could get out of the contract was if her father were challenged and lost the fight. The winner would become the new alpha. As the pack's alpha he could take any bride he wanted under the law and no one could question his choice.

Gwen was surprised by how much it bothered her to see him leave. It wasn't as if they were friends, he was the pilot and she was his passenger. Now that he had delivered her to her father, he was no longer concerned. She sighed and followed her father into the cabin.

"I'm going to put your bag in your room. Dinner is ready, we were waiting for you to arrive. We expected you a couple of hours earlier."

"I expected to be here earlier. The pilot was late so we left late."

She followed him back into the main room of the cabin and sat down in the chair he indicated. Gwen did her best to ignore his friend as he lowered his enormous bulk into the chair next to her at the table. He could easily have chosen the chair across from her or at the far end of the table, instead of squeezing in beside her.

Almost immediately an attractive older woman began bringing in dishes of food. The aromas wafting through the air had her mouth watering. Normally a picky eater, Gwen was surprised by how hungry she was. The deer meat was cooked perfectly, medium rare as she preferred. And there was plenty of it. She cut her eyes at Otto before taking the chair at the end of the table.

During the meal, her father continued to ply her with questions, asking about her mother, her last few years, and what she was doing now. She answered his questions but wondered why so many? Most of the information he already knew. It reminded her of a job interview.

Otto, her father's friend listened to everything she said to her father without comment. Gwen could sense his displeasure over some of the answers she gave her father.

Morgan, the woman who had cooked the dinner, turned out to be her grandmother. Another unexpected bit of information that would have been nice to know as she was growing up. There was a moment or two when Morgan was so surprised by one of her father's questions she fought back a smirk but other than a raised eyebrow or a snort of amusement, she said nothing.

After Morgan cleared the table, she brought out a cake and a pot of coffee, setting them in from of Gwen along with cups and saucers.

"I take cream with my coffee," Otto said. He looked at her as if daring her to say something.

That's when she realized he expected her to serve the cake and coffee. Gwen bit her lip but refrained from telling the arrogant ass to get it himself.

Before she could reply, her father said. "Coffee sounds good to me. Would you pour, dear? I will slice the cake."

He was her father's guest and it was easier to simply pour the coffee than to fight an unimportant battle. She slid the cream pitcher over between the two men and poured them both cups of the steaming beverage. She still had tea remaining from her dinner and preferred that not really being a big fan of coffee. She was wondering when his guest planned on leaving. His presence was making it difficult to talk to her father about certain subjects.

After seven years, the reality of how her father looked had shaken her. Her memory was of a strong, handsome man who protected her from the cruelty of the world. Her perception had changed and now she saw an aging man who would soon need someone to care for him. His smile had taken her back to the last time she saw him He had taken her to the park near our apartment. He had sat on a see-saw like he was one of the neighborhood kids, staring up at the sparkling stars as we went up and down. Gwen wiped a lone tear from her cheek. There had been a shooting star, a shining beautiful light that darted across the eastern sky leaving a white trail to mark its existence. They had both made a wish, then laughed because they both knew it was never going to happen. Her mother had made her choice and never went backward. Her mother's time with her father had ended many years ago. The gods never heard that wish, or at least if they did, they didn't grant it. He had stopped visiting after that. She had heard he had married, a widow with two children. She figured the kids would have moved out by now. They were both older than her. Until Ty had mentioned his aunt dying, she had believed that like her mother, she had divorced him, too.

Either way, she knew she wanted to be alone for a while so she could absorb everything. After about an hour she gave up and made her excuses. "I'm really tired. I think I'm going to call it a night."

Her father nodded. "That's fine dear. We can talk in the morning. I have a lot I need to discuss with you."

Gwen was curious but not enough to suffer through another moment with his guest. "Goodnight Mr. Witt. It was nice meeting you. I hope to see you again before I leave."

He broke out laughing. She wondered what he thought was so funny, but not enough to remain in the room. For the first time since she was a little girl, she locked her bedroom door behind her.

Chapter 3

Gwen awoke suddenly, certain someone was watching her. Since her room was on the second floor, unless her voyeuristic admirer enjoyed climbing trees there was little chance anyone was out there. Wearing nothing but her cotton pajama's she slipped from the bed and padded across the room to the bathroom. She flipped on the overhead light beside the mirror over the sink and gaped at the disheveled woman looking back from the reflective glass. Her wavy auburn hair was a tangled mess. The makeup she'd been too lazy to remove the night before was faded and smeared around both eyes, making her look like an exhausted caricature of a raccoon. This is got to go. She opened a jar of cold crème she had in her overnight bag and used tissue paper to wipe the smeared mascara from under her eyes. There was not a lot she could do for her hair, so she brushed it straight and pulled it back into a tight ponytail. She thought about moisturizing but decided she had no one to impress. Her father probably wouldn't even notice the pillow marks and fine lines around her eyes.

She was surprised to find him waiting in an antique rocker at the foot of the stairs. He pulled her tight and whispered in her ear, "I am so glad you came."

Kate kissed him gently on the cheek. "It's good to be here," she murmured as she followed him down the hall, noticing how the white painted cabinetry, red-checked curtains, and white subway tiled backsplash made the traditional kitchen look cozy and inviting.

Morgan was bustling around the room, preparing a traditional country breakfast, complete with pancakes and bacon.

Gwen's stomach rumbled, reminding her of how little she had managed to get down during dinner the night before. She followed her nose toward three loaves of freshly baked bread sitting on the counter near the stove. Before Gwen could ask, Morgan cut her a thick slice and was loading it with butter and homemade strawberry jam. She settled down at the table and nibbled on the bread while Morgan scrambled her eggs to go with the bacon and pancakes. There was no way she could eat like this for long, but for now, she was going to enjoy every bite.

Her father must have smelled the coffee or the bread because he joined her at the table as Morgan began setting down the plates.

As if he could read her mind his stomach growled.

She laughed. "So what is the plan for the day."

He stopped pouring his syrup and answered," Catching up. We have a lot to talk about. I have left word we are not to be disturbed. I figured we would go fishing like we used to before things changed.

Gwen smiled. Fishing sounded great to her. Most of her favorite memories were from their family fishing trips. She was as excited about it as she had been as a child.

***

"So catch me up on the exciting life of Gwen Marlow…"

Gwen had whiled away the entire afternoon hiking and talking with her father. As they walked along, she could feel the stresses of her day to day life melting away. He was really happy in the little private kingdom and he wanted her to know everything about it. He shared gossip about the more colorful residents, personal stories both good and bad that he had been involved in. When they reached the lake he shared a few of his precious insider secrets, such as expert advice on fishing for catfish and the spots on the river where the biggest trout could be found. She could not remember a time she enjoyed herself more. Except…something kept nagging at her subconscious. Whenever she tried to turn the conversation to his life there on the mountain, he avoided the question and changed the subject. About all she could find out was he had to buy feed this year because it was so dry. With the government keeping the price for beef down this year; having to buy feed could wipe out small farmers. Not that he was a small farmer, his farm had to be several hundred acres, maybe more.

Now her father was watching a trail of dark gray storm clouds that had morphed into angry thunderheads. "We might better start heading back toward the cabin. It looks like it's about ready to let loose."

They began walking back up the trail but it was clear the rain would arrive before they reached the cabin. They had just passed the barn at the lower edge of the cow pasture when the thunderclouds burst free and released a torrent of water, soaking them both in a matter of seconds.

Morgan was standing at the door watching as they came running for the porch. "Land sakes Gideon, why didn't you shift when you saw the storm coming? You know the doctor said you need to avoid getting chilled."

Gideon was shaking his head at Morgan with a panicked look in his eyes.

Gwen knew him well enough to know when he was hiding something. She took the towel Morgan passed her and dried her hair, then changed into dry clothes before going back downstairs.

Her father was waiting in the Den, a resigned expression on his face. It was apparent he had made some type of a decision, and that decision involved what she had heard. His eyes stayed locked on hers as she walked to the chair across from him and sat down. She could tell something was amiss, there was a heaviness in his posture and his usual ease was gone. Finally, he rested his head in his hands and took a haggard breath before speaking. 'I've been avoiding this conversation for much too long already. Time is up and I need to tell you a few things...things that you are going to have trouble believing."

He locked his eyes with hers and she could see how much this conversation was taking out of him. It must be something serious, mother stroke serious. Was he dying?

"I know you love to read books. You prefer mysteries, but occasionally I remember seeing you with a fantasy book in your hands. Maybe one of the Narnia books?"

She smiled. It had been many years since she had read that series. She was surprised he remembered.

"Well, you know how there were two kinds of animals, the dumb beasts and the talking beasts?"

She could see he was struggling with what he was trying to say, so she simply nodded.

"Would you believe parts of that story is true?" he paused, expecting some type of response, anger, laughter, hysteria, something. Instead, she sat quietly, as if she was unsure what he wanted from her.

She appeared to be thinking but all she said was, "Okay."

He sighed. "Gwen, I'm not entirely human. Neither are you." He watched as a series of expressions flashed across her face before finally settling back into her natural calm appearance. He could tell she was struggling to keep the smile hidden, but it was just behind the tight lips.

"So, what are we then?"

He stood up. "This is important. You turn eighteen tomorrow. I should have told you years ago, so you could have taken time to absorb all this before your eighteenth birthday. But your mother almost died and I avoided the confrontation. Keep an open mind and don't freak." He stepped away from her, standing behind the chair. She saw him lay his shirt across the back of the chair and then his pants. She couldn't see him but she knew he was naked. "Ugh…dad, you being naked is kinda making me uncomfortable."

"Just keep an open mind." He ducked down behind the chair, and seconds later, first one, then another large black paw appeared on the back of the chair. Slowly, inch by inch the head of an extremely large cream-colored cat came into view. It stood there looking over at her for a moment, then with effortless ease it bounded over the back of the chair, landing in front of her.

"Exhale. You can't keep holding your breath."

She hit the floor.

***

Gwen woke up alone in her bedroom. She knew there was something important she needed to remember but her mind felt fuzzy. No matter how hard she tried to remember what happened she blanked. It had something to do with her father. It was as if a light had gone off. He wasn't human! He was some kind of lion except he was more light brown than gold and had no mane. A cougar... that's what they called it. Maybe it was some kind of elaborate scheme? She never saw him change. He was down behind a chair. Maybe the big cat is a pet and he taught it to sit with its feet on the back of the chair. Why he would play such a stupid trick on her, she didn't know. Then she remembered the voice in her head. That wasn't a trick. She was about to go back downstairs and talk to him when there a knock on the door.

"Are you awake," Morgan asked.

Gwen had a feeling she knew the answer to that question already. "Yes. Come in."

"I brought you a tray. You didn't have dinner."

"Thank you, I am a bit hungry." She was starving. Over the last few weeks, her appetite had been growing. The salads she had always enjoyed didn't take the edge off her hunger. Now she wanted meat. She had figured it was an iron deficiency and started taking vitamins. Now she wondered if it had anything to do with her father's proclamation.

Morgan sat the tray on the table by the bed and pulled up a chair. "Your father didn't do a very good job of explaining things. I figured I might be able to help."

Gwen looked at her and noticed she had hazel eyes similar to hers. Then her eyes changed, with the pupils becoming more elongated like a cat. They stayed that way until she reacted, then as if certain she had seen the change, they shifted back to the normal round pupil.

"You are like him?"

"Yes. This is why your father wanted you here for your eighteenth birthday. He was afraid you would not be able to handle the shift on your own. To be honest, we are not sure if you will shift at all. You are half-human, and not every one of the mixed blood can change into their cat."

"So there are other half cats. I'm not the only one?" Gwen figured she needed to get as much information as possible before she decided what to do next.

"No, you are definitely not the only one." She smiled, trying to ease the tension in the room. "I know you have lots of doubts. I'm here to answer any question you feel you need to be answered. Do you have any?

What did she need to know? She was still struggling to wrap her mind around the idea of her father changing into a mountain lion. Now they expected her to accept the idea that she might do it, too.

"What are we? Aliens?" There had been rumors of UFOs for as long as human records had been kept. Egypt worshiped a woman with a cat head, so why not? Of course, they also worshiped a man with a dog head. Did that mean some people could change into dogs, too?

"Yes, there are wolf shifters. Among others."

Gwen was startled. She had not asked that question out loud. Morgan had heard her. How? Now that she was paying attention, she realized Morgan wasn't speaking out loud. Could everyone talk mind to mind?

"It's related to the blood tie. You must be closely related for it to work. Even then it's not always possible. I just happen to be especially skilled in telepathy. Your father inherited it from me."

"From you? That makes you my grandmother?"

"Yes dear, that is correct. When my husband died I moved in with my son. He neglected to mention he had a half-human daughter until a few years ago. It was a surprise to us all."

"Surprise? Mom and I thought you were dead." "Thanks dad," she thought. "I missed out on having a grandmother growing up. It would have been nice."

Morgan smiled and Gwen realized she had heard that, too. "The shift is not difficult however you must remain calm. You will need to concentrate on being human to switch back. Keep your human form locked in your mind at all times."

"What happens if I can't?"

"I will be with you and I can help. So can you father. Sometimes you fall asleep as a wolf and wake as a human. Sometimes it's reversed. That's why it was so important to bring you home. You need people like you around you now."

"Wait. Is everyone in the area a Cat?"

"Almost everyone. The ones who aren't, are distant relations." She pushed the tray towards Gwen and switched back to talking. "Go ahead and eat. You have a lot to think about. Once you get your head wrapped around everything, come downstairs and talk to your father."

Morgan stood and walked toward the door. Gwen noticed how easily she moved for an old woman. It was more of a glide or a slink. Like a cat. She wondered how she had missed it earlier. Her grandmother! What else had been hidden from her? Her stomach growled again, reminding her that she needed to eat. She picked up the sandwich and took a bite. Roast beef, rare. Piled high between two thin slices of bread. There had to be half a pound of meat. She ate every bite. She leaned back against the pillow on the bed and thought about everything she had learned. Despite her best effort tears formed in her eyes. She closed her eyes, willing herself to not cry because once she started it would be impossible to stop the flow of tears. She hated showing weakness. Maybe she had inherited that from her father too. She let out a shaky breath and used a tissue to dry her face. She wasn't sure how much time passed before she decided it was time to face her father again.

He had the decency to look embarrassed.

"Sit down. I guess you have a lot of questions." He patted the sofa next to him but she chose the chair instead.

"A hundred thousand or so," she replied. "Like… did my mother know?"

"Yes. She knew I was a shifter. And that there was a possibility you would be one, too. That's one of the things that broke us up. She had no intention of leaving the city and moving to a small town in the mountains. She loved her job. And I was proud of her, not many women could be an 'A' level actress and raise a child on her own." He grinned, "especially one as inquisitive as you. You were always trying things that could have gotten you in serious trouble… or worse. We used to joke about you needed nine lives. Too bad the folk tale got it wrong. We only have one life, like a human."

"That sucks. It was one of the better characteristics I was looking forward to."

This time he laughed. That sound made her feel better. He was her father, and if he could turn into a mountain lion, then it couldn't be that bad.

"So what are we exactly?"

"That's a complicated answer. When I change I am darker in color than a lot of the others. There are jokes about an ancestor mating with a jaguar. Since the Jaguar is almost extinct in the US it had to have been several generations ago. Most of the pride had the typical golden brown coloring of cougars but some are darker, almost grey and some have spots like a jaguar. Until you shift there is no way to know what your coloring will be."

"So I'm a real life cougar, and not because I want to date men much younger than me?"

"That's a subject for another time. Let's stick to shifting for now. While you may not have nine lives, being able to change your shape does have good points. Your body heals itself much faster than a human."

"A human. Are we not humans?"

"Well, you are at least half-human. We are not sure where our bloodline started. There have been stories of Skinwalkers throughout history. It's also possible we are descended from a naturally occurring breed of animals. Another possibility is that the ability came from somewhere other than Earth. No one is sure."

"So we are like werewolves?"

"No. While there are wolf shifters, they are not usually killers. Werewolves are wolf shifters with rabies. The virus infects their brains, driving them to do things they would not normally do. We kill any we find in that condition. So do the wolves."

"Explain something to me. Why did you wait until now to let me know this?"

He got that same hang-dog expression, the one he always got when he had done something he didn't want to talk about. "That's something I am ashamed of. I should have told you years ago. When your mother had her stroke, I should have brought you here. Put your mother in a home nearby. Instead, I started drinking and stayed away. My drinking drove my wife away; she knew about your mother and you. I would have married her, I loved her. But my marriage to Anola was arranged by my father and we do not divorce. Anola was my life mate. She was never happy because she knew about my other family. My human family."

That explained a lot of things, like why my last name was Marlow and not Wolf. I had my mother's name because he was already married. "Do you have any other children?" She felt like she already knew the answer to that question. She remembered Ty saying something about that on the trip over. He mentioned being related by marriage. He had called Morgan his aunt. That meant Anola was related to Tyrel through his mother. Her half brother and sister were his cousins. Did that make Tyrel a shifter? He had been undeniably evasive about the mountain.

"Two. My daughter is married. My son is in college. He is only a year older than you."

She took a deep breath and asked the question she needed answering but was afraid to hear. " Who is Otto Witt?"

Chapter 4

Dinner that night was a tense one. Until the dirty dishes were clear and her father's third bottle of beer was opened no one talked much. The house phone rang and Gideon excused himself to answer it. He disappeared for several minutes. Now that Gwen knew who she was, Morgan had joined them for dinner and she was doing her best to keep a casual conversation flowing in his absence. Every so often her father's voice would grow louder, but he was too far away for Gwen to make out any words.

When he returned, he sat at the table and rested his head in his hands for a few moments before speaking. "Otto will be dropping by in a few minutes. He wants to ride along with us while I show Gwen the town."

Morgan rolled her eyes but she did not comment.

Gwen was not especially happy but she could not come up with an excuse to get out of the sightseeing excursion. Her father's truck had a bench seat but being squashed in between him and Otto over an extended period of time was not something she was looking forward to. "Maybe we should wait for another day to look around town."

Her father looked frustrated as he shook his head. "I need to talk to a few people anyway. Otto can keep you company while I am taking care of Pride business."

Much sooner than she hoped Otto pulled his little Toyota Pickup into the yard and parked it next to her father's full size F-150. Gwen cringed as he slid out from behind the wheel and wobbled toward the cabin.

Just as she expected, once again Otto smelled of sour beer and sweat. His clothes were the same ones he had been wearing when she arrived the day before. The blackish-grey sweat ring around his neck was tinged green from the cheap chain he was wearing, another sign that he rarely bothered to bathe and if he did he never bothered to scrub his neck. She was willing to bet the grey tinged socks that peeked out from beneath the skin-tight jogging pants were supposed to be white.

The ride to the location of her father's business meeting' took ten minutes and in her mind, that was nine and a half minutes too long. Otto used her leg as his armrest, laying his heavy forearm along her thigh and wrapping his meaty hand around her knee. When they while driving through town they passed the small community store where Tyrel had stopped for a coke. For the briefest moment she faced an irrational impulse to jump out and run. With her father on one side and Otto on the other, it wasn't likely she would manage to get out of the truck, so she resigned herself to the undesirable state of affairs and didn't try the reckless escape attempt.

About a half a mile past the center of the small town was a cement block building about twice as big as a convenience store. The sign outside displayed the words Sit -N-Sip in faded letters along with a painting of two overflowing beer mugs. Brightly colored neon signs advertised the more popular brands. The bright red 'open' sign flashed on and off. From the number of cars and trucks packed into the parking lot, it appeared to be a very popular spot to have a few drinks and spend time with friends.

Gwen slid out of the truck behind her father and was prepared to go inside when he stopped her. "You are not old enough to go inside. The law says twenty-one and while they might look the other way because you are my daughter, it's not the kind of place I would want you to patronize. Wait out here with Otto, I won't be gone long."

Gwen started to protest, then realized it would not do any good. When the truck door on the other side opened and shut she hoped Otto intended to head inside with her father. Instead he walked over to join her.

"I figured we could get to know each other a little more," he said as he leaned against the cab beside her.

"Not likely, I have already seen enough to know I'm not interested. I think it best if you direct your attention to someone else." He might be her father's friend, but that did not mean she had to spend any time with him. She turned, intending to climb back in the truck and lock the doors. Before she realized what he planned to do, he had locked his fingers around her wrist. Her temper flared white-hot and she whirled toward him, slamming his body back against the side of the truck. Her sudden move took him by surprise, and he lost his grip on her arm.

"Don't touch me," she snarled. She turned to walk away, not caring where she went as long as it was away from him.

"We're not through talking." Otto grabbed her ponytail as she began walking, using it to jerk her backward into his arms. Once he pulled her close, he swiveled and used his weight to push her body up against the side of her father's truck. One of his knees was jammed between her legs and his free hand gripped her roughly by the jaw. She tried shoving him away as he crushed her lips with his, trying to force his tongue into her mouth. When that didn't work, she stomped down on his foot, desperate to escape his grasp. He growled softly, growing irritated by her struggles as he attempted to slide his hand up under her blouse. His sweaty hand pawed at her bra, groping and squeezing her breast so hard she whimpered. He took the slight sound to be submission and tore the expensive pink lace fabric away. Now certain he would not stop, she plunged her teeth deep into his bottom lip, cutting into the tissue. The taste of warm blood goaded his anger. He slapped her, knocking her to the ground at his feet.

His finger went to his lip and he stared at the blood dripping down the side before glaring at her, yellow fire flickering in his eyes.

"Bitch. You'll pay for that." He lunged toward her, both hands wrapping tightly around her throat, intending to teach her who was in charge. She clawed at him, but nothing she tried would loosen his grip. Somehow she forced out a weak scream.

Seconds later she saw her father grab Otto and slam him to the ground.

Otto looked up at him and snarled, "What? She's mine. You signed the contract. Best she learns her place now. Tonight or tomorrow after the ceremony, either way, she will be my mine."

What ceremony? What did he think she was doing tomorrow? There was no way in Hell she was going anywhere close to the greasy Neanderthal, tomorrow or any other day. She stared at her father but he would not look her in the eyes. What contract was he talking about? What else had her father forgotten to mention?

Her father whispered something to Otto that shut him up. His eyes shifted back to Gwen and she shivered. She could see the implied threat reflected there and it scared her. He stood up and dusted his clothes off, then walked back into the bar.

"Get in the truck. I will be right back." Her father followed Otto back into the bar.

Gwen thought about walking but decided that was not a realistic choice. Instead, she got into the truck and locked all the doors. There was no way that fat bastard was getting back in the truck with her. If her father insisted on giving him a ride home, she was riding in the back of the truck. Several people had rushed outside when her father had, and they were watching her. At any other time, she would have expected witnesses to come to her assistance. These people acted like a woman got molested in the parking lot all the time.

She had needed to go to the bathroom and walked toward the bar, hoping it might be safe to enter long enough to use the facilities. Her father's voice in shadows not far from the door caught her attention.

"…never listen to anything. You had to get impatient and start pawing at her like a teenager in heat. If you screwed this up, you have only yourself to blame. You could have waited until after the ceremony. Once she shifts she will go into heat, and gladly would have accepted you. Now we are …" The voices faded into the distance.

Gwen thought about following them. Then she remembered her father changing. She was fairly certain Otto could do the same thing. One cougar was bad, two would be impossible to deal with. She regretted leaving her pistol at home in her luggage.

She could just make out what Otto was saying, "--- the contract. Make certain she is dressed and ready for the ceremony in the morning. I will be there to drive her to the gathering at nine." This time Otto did not wait for Gideon's response. Instead, he walked back into the bar with his two friends. Her father stood there alone for a moment.

Gwen turned and ran back toward the truck. At least she didn't have to pee anymore. If her father asked about her wet jeans, she would blame it on Otto's attack. She had certainly been scared enough then. She headed back to the truck, locked the doors and waited.

Her father made excuses for him when he returned alone. "Otto is going to hang around and shoot some pool. He sends his apologies and hopes you will forgive him for losing his head over a beautiful woman. He will get a ride home with a friend."

Forgive him? Not likely. He's lucky he has friends.

"We need to talk anyway," she said.

On the way back to the cabin they had another discussion and this time she did not let him weasel out and give her half an answer. Her father explained what Otto meant by his ceremony comment and the answer had been as bad as she feared.

"I wish I had a good excuse for everything but I don't. I have a problem with alcohol. "

Gwen grew quiet as he spoke. It seemed that her father not only drank like a fish; he also liked to gamble and often lost. During one especially serious drinking spree he had been betting large amounts, expecting a big return on what he thought was a perfect hand after a string of bad luck. He had run out of cash and he offered the pot an IOU. A big IOU. Twenty-five thousand dollars. He was so convinced he could not loose he didn't take another card. When everyone had placed their bets or folded, he had proudly laid out his hand, four sixes, with a queen boot. Only to find out Otto also had four of a kind. Four Aces, and a Queen boot. Feeling the world opening up beneath him and the fires of Hell beckoning, Gideon had stumbled away from the table and disappeared into the night.

Two days later Otto had shown up at the cabin with the IOU. He asked when he could pick up the money and her father had to admit he didn't have it. He would need to sell off some of his assets to raise the cash. He offered stock in the ski resort but Otto had no interest in owning part of a tourist attraction.

Then Otto asked about the photo on his desk. When Gideon explained it was his daughter, he had asked how old his daughter was.

"In the photo she's almost thirteen. I haven't seen her for five years."

"So she's almost eighteen and unmarried?" His voice quivered in his excitement as he began to formulate a plan in his mind. Gideon's stepson was two souled and attended college on the west coast. Before marrying his stepdaughter had attended an all-female college in New York. Otto wasn't sure if she preferred dating the same sex like her brother, but he had never seen her with a man until he saw photos of her wedding. Neither had children. Nor had they shown any interest in following in their stepfather's footsteps.

Gideon was surprised when Otto offered him a way out of the debt. A way out that included Gwen. He had signed a contract betrothing her to Otto, a contract due to be concluded on her eighteenth birthday, …tomorrow.

So far the day leading up to her birthday had been anything but happy. One the way home her father had stopped at the local store to pick up a few things Morgan had ordered and she remained in the truck. Gwen lay her head against the glass of the truck door and closed her eyes. So much to take in. Such a short time to absorb it. The idea of being a half breed shifter had been hard enough to accept. Since then she had also learned her father is the clan leader of the Pride. That did not fit in with her mental image of Gideon. The father she grew up with was a truck driver who stayed on the road all the time. When would he have time to take care of an entire pride of giant cats? Well, pumas or panthers or cougars or whatever the hell they are. He couldn't even find the time to visit her twice a year.

As if that wasn't crazy enough, then he hits her with the idea that she was going to change into one of them. Yeah, sure she was. He really expected her to accept the idea of being some kind of whacked-out werecat, marry the pathetic mate chosen by bad luck and calmly bear his kittens. In other words to be a "good little mountain wife". Fuck that.

Instead of heading straight back to the cabin, he had driven around the mountain resort explaining that she would inherit everything once he passed on. Except she wouldn't really be inheriting anything. Instead, she was expected to turn over all control to the sweaty hands of her chosen mate. He could keep his ski lodge. Maybe he could bribe one of the other women in the Pride with it. There was not enough money in the state to make her let that pig touch her again. She pulled her backpack out of the closet and began shoving her things inside. As soon as they fell asleep she was out of there.

Gwen could still hear the talking points her father had prepared running through the back of her mind. He must have planned it ahead of time, working out what he would say when he had the opportunity. He had listed off what he considered important virtues in a mate. "Otto will be the pack Alpha after me. He is the best match you could hope for. He may not be a handsome human, but he is a strong, muscular cougar that will keep the Pride well in hand. "He must have realized she wasn't receptive to his

Gwen sat silently, with her arms crossed tightly against her chest, thinking Please don't let him extol Otto's virtues to me… again! Thank goodness he didn't. The creep made her sick to her stomach. There was no way she was going to marry him.

His final plea had broken her heart. "It's not just me that will suffer from your refusal. I can't sell the Ski resort, it's already mortgaged. To get the money, I will have to sell off this part of the mountain. People who have lived here all their lives will have to leave their homes. Morgan will lose her home. The town will die. Most of the land the Pride lives on belongs to me. So you are not just hurting me, you are hurting everyone."

As soon as they pulled into the yard, she jumped out and headed for her bedroom, thinking he would take the hint. Instead, he followed her to the front porch and asked her to give him an answer before she went inside.

Gwen took a deep breath and prepared to tell him where he shove it when she spotted Morgan watching from the doorway. She had just found out she had a grandmother. There was no way she could hurt her. "I will marry him to save your ass but after that, we are through. You are no longer my father. Once the debt is paid I will get a divorce.

His face fell. This surprised her as he appeared upset. It was the first time she recalled ever seeing that much pain in his golden brown eyes. "Divorce is not an option. We mate for life! Once you accept him, you will be bonded until one of you die."

Her eyes darkened and her voice grew tight and shrill. " I never thought I would feel this way, but I hate you." She could feel his eyes on her as she climbed the stairs. She didn't look back.

***

Gwen's mind was filled with conflicting emotions. She was mentally and physically exhausted. After picking up the groceries had even driven by the church where they expected her to be bonded. Everything was already arranged. The invitations had been sent out weeks earlier.

He had asked her, "Would you like to talk to the minister before the ceremony tomorrow?"

She shook her head no. There was no way she was going to walk into that building voluntarily; they would have to drag her inside with her kicking and screaming all the way. God would strike her down if he got wind of what she was thinking. She felt like a total hypocrite. She had always believed in God or at least some kind of all mighty being who created everything. She loved the feeling of peace and love she felt in Church. Her only issue with religion was the people. So many of them dressed up in their best clothes like it was a fashion show. Once they were all decked out they sat in the chapel while the minister lectured them, before demanding payment for his time. Church had always seemed like a business to her. Her mother had not been especially religious, she had sent Gwen to Sunday School and Vacation Bible School until she was old enough to get a part-time job on the weekends. After that it was never mentioned.

Gwen had always felt like sending her to church was her mother's way of getting to sleep late on Sunday mornings. Right now Gwen wasn't very happy with God, and her father could kiss her ass. There was no way she was marrying Otto. If he looked into her heart, God would understand. She wasn't certain her father would.

Morgan had come to the room earlier. She had set on the bed beside and announced, "Gwen, I need to tell you more about your first heat."

"You're a little late. I've been having my period since I was thirteen. And I lost my virginity my first semester in college." It was sweet of her to try to fill in for my mother but thinking about Otto and his hands on my body made me more uncomfortable.

"That's not quite the same thing. There is so much more to it than sex."

Gwen didn't want to listen, but her curiosity won out and she couldn't resist. She was interested in learning everything she could about her cougar bloodline and while her grandmother wasn't exactly warm and cuddly, she seemed to have Gwen's best interest in her heart.

"Once you have begun to shift your body will start changing. Your muscles will grow stronger. You will feel the urge to run and jump and hunt. Some women take weeks or months to feel their first heat. Others feel it come on within hours of their first shift. There is no way to know what yours will be like."

She paused, seemingly seeking the right words. "Have you ever had a yeast infection?"

"Yes, once. That itch will drive you crazy."

"When your heat first comes on, you won't notice until you're around a male. It will be worse than that itch, your tissue will swell and you will feel the need to rut. You will grow increasingly agitated, sensitive and snappy until you …scratch the itch. If this happens and Otto is the only male around, you will not only accept him; it will be all you can do to stop yourself from throwing him on the ground and taking him."

Gwen felt a wave of revulsion wash over her. She could not imagine wanting that man to touch her.

"I had always hoped that you would find your life mate and be happy. Otto is not and will never be your mate. After the ceremony he will be bonded by our law. That bond gives him the right to scratch your itch when you are in heat. Luckily, that only happens twice a year. The rest of the time the decision is your own."

"Some choice."

"It is unfortunate that humanity does not know about our people. For your safety, you must be with your people tomorrow. You will not be able to stop the transformation when it happens. And it will happen, I can sense the changes beginning in your body already." Morgan glanced at the clock on the table. Eight after twelve. It was her birthday.

Gwen nodded. She could feel something happening already. No urge to change into an animal, but she felt healthier, stronger. Somehow she needed to make Morgan believe she was accepting her limited choices. She yawned.

Morgan's right eyebrow quirked but she didn't question Gwen's exhaustion. "Try and get some sleep. You are going to have a long day tomorrow." Morgan pulled the door shut behind her. Gwen could hear her turning a key in the lock. She would go down to the kitchen to speak to her father, maybe eat some pie and drink coffee while they talked. Morgan was convinced Gwen understood the importance of being with her people at this momentous time.

Gwen had no idea how she was going to get out of the contract but somehow she had to figure it out. In the morning, her life would be over. Forget college, it was doubtful she would be allowed to go to Walmart on her own.

Because of a stupid card game, she would be forced into a marriage with an animal. No, Otto was lower than that, calling him an animal was an insult to mountain lions. It didn't matter that the idea of marrying him made her sick, they would force her to go through with the ceremony and then lock her into a building with him until she went into heat. At that point, she wouldn't care as long as his cock was hard.

She was not a product to barter away. If she intended to get away, she didn't have much time. Just being in the room left her feeling smothered. She opened the window and felt better, enjoying the scent of honeysuckle on the breeze. Excitement built in her chest as she realized what was happening. She was going to change.

Gwen slipped out of her pajamas and dressed in the jeans and tee-shirt she had laid out. Instead of her usual shoes, she slid her feet into the same hiking boots she had worn earlier. She was leaving her luggage behind. And her purse. It was sitting on the counter downstairs. She had purposely left her phone on the charger and her purse in plain sight. Her cash, credit card and driver's license were in her pocket. She was certain her father had placed a camera with an alarm on the stairs. They were expecting her to try to leave but figured she would wait until everyone was asleep. That was a mistake.

There was a convenient tree growing outside her window. She would need to make a short jump, maybe five feet or so, and catch hold of a limb to prevent a fall, but she had jumped much farther. Her time spent rock climbing with Michael last summer was going to come in handy. Few women would have attempted to reach the tree. No one in the house would be expecting her to leave that way. In less than a moment she was standing on the ground beside the tree.

There was an old truck they used to deliver feed to the cows sitting by the barn. She knew where Gideon kept the keys.

The moonlight did not give off enough light for her to see which key was which, so she had to identify the key by touch. Her hands were shaking as she slid the key into the slot and turned it. The engine turned over a few times but would not engage. After several attempts, it became obvious the truck was not going to start. "Damn you!" She smacked the steering wheel, jerked the keys from the ignition and looked around for another vehicle. The yard was empty of anything except Gideon's truck. It required a key-fob, and her father kept it hooked on his belt. There would be no escape that way.

The trail through the pasture was her best option. She began running.

Chapter 5

Soft sunlight streaming through the cedar trees coaxed Gwen from a restless sleep. She could not believe she had fallen asleep in a clearing that way. Anyone hunting her in cat form could have followed her scent directly to her makeshift bower. The cool breeze coming off the crest of the mountain cut through her t-shirt, making her wish she had thought to bring a jacket or a sweater. She must be relatively high up in the mountains, a bank of low clouds hung between the valley peaks. By the amount of moisture she could feel, it might have had been raining in the valley below her. This was great, the rain would wash away any scent she might have left, making it difficult to follow her. Last night she had run out of trail. Faced with an unexpected decision she began working her way upward, climbing the smaller rock faces in the moonlight. Eventually, the cloud cover had blocked out the moonlight and she had to stop. Locating this clearing had been fortunate, it was surrounded by large boulders on three sides, giving her a sense of security. Despite the large rocks and the cedar trees the tiny open space felt compact, not closed off or claustrophobic. It reminded her of sleeping in her mother's arms, a sheltered, safe sanctuary. She did not remember falling asleep.

Without a clock, all she could do is guess the time. By now her father had discovered her ruse and realized she had no intention of marrying Otto. As Alpha of the Pride, he would have the right to call in trackers, sending them out in various directions to try and find her location. Her only hope was their lack of information. Her father considered her a city girl, used to luxuries and soft living. They would spend most of their time searching along the roadways in hopes of cutting her trail. Her father would naturally send men over to the Ski Lodge to ask around. It was way too early in the fall for snow, there would not be a lot of vacationers there. She had considered heading that way. Then her logical mind had screamed 'no' in no uncertain terms, and for once she had listened. She had made the trip to the lake using the same path her father had walked with her. Once she arrived at the lake, she had waded along the shoreline until she reached the creek. At that point she had two options, following the creek downstream and hoping it would lead to a road, or heading upstream until she reached the source of the water. This time she did the opposite of logic and went upstream.

She walked back to the creek, washed his face in the crisp, cold water, and weighed her options from this point. She would need to find food somewhere. Water would be no issue, there were creeks everywhere. If she were lower down toward the lake, she would easily find fish and crustaceans to eat. She had noticed crayfish scuttling away earlier. Since she had slept only ten feet or so from the creek, the chances of anyone cutting her trail were extremely low. But once she began moving cross country the odds would improve in their favor.

Morgan's words were nagging at her. It was her birthday. She was going to change. She knew it as well as she knew her name. She might be half-human, but her father's genes were dominant. She knew instinctively that she would shift easily. She could do it now if she wanted. This intrigued her. She was certain she could travel faster in her cat form. There was something she needed to do before she made the shift. She removed her clothes. The tee shirt had long sleeves, and this would make it easier. She tied the neck of the shirt closed with a small knot. After rolling her pants around her boots, she used her socks to ensure they stayed together. Then she dropped them into her tee-shirt after first tying the tail of the shirt together, then tying the two sleeves together. Her makeshift pack was ready. Now she had to shift.

Her father had told her she needed to keep her human shape in mind to shift back. Perhaps that meant she needed to picture her body as a cougar to change to her cat form. She wasn't a hundred percent sure what a mountain lion looked like. Her father's face peeking over the chair was a start, she pictured a slightly smaller, more feminine head, with tawny brown fur instead of her father's black. Their bodies would be similar, but much larger than a house cat, with heavier muscles. She took a deep breath and concentrated.

She was certain she was on the right track as her skin tingled and her pelt began to sprout. Her confidence wavered when the first jolts of pain hit her as her bones began to lengthen and bend into a new shape. The muscles in her back and stomach tightened, some becoming shorter, others longer. She did not notice when she fell to the ground, overcome by pain as the bones in her face contorted, forming into the slimmer, slightly elongated jaws and long sharp teeth of the big cat. Finally, her fingers and toes shortened, her nails thickening into razor sharp claws.

As the pain ended she rose to her feet and began to move…first in a slow walk and then trotting and finally a distance eating lope. She only made it a short distance when she remembered the pack she had made. Returning to the clearing, she picked up the bundle by the tied arms and began running along the ground, moving parallel to the mountain top. She wanted to climb the mountains. She wanted to run through the fields and hunt in the forest. A rabbit cutting across the clearing caught her eye and she realized she was hungry. But that could wait. She was a cougar and it felt great!

Several times she had bounded up upon boulders that would have required her to climb or detour around. She had no idea where she was going, only the knowledge that anywhere was better than remaining in the area for Otto or her father to find. Morgan's words stayed with her. She would go into heat soon. When that happened, any available male would be the right male. Somehow she had to assure herself the choice would be hers and not her hormones. This meant being around other cat shifters. Other than her father and Otto, she only knew one attractive man that might be a shifter. She needed to find Tyrel.

***

After hours of wandering unknown trails and random climbs, Gwen finally reached the base of a limestone crag and ascended to a flat granite overlook. Her head swiveled to the left and right as her eyes sought any type of familiarity amongst the vibrant beauty. From the overlook she could see for miles in every direction, and everywhere she looked she saw acres and acres of unmolested, lush, mountain terrain. If there was any sign of buildings they were hidden by the heavy growth of trees. To the north, she could see a narrow stream that zigzagged through the steep valley walls. She had no memory of traveling through a valley. To the south, the creek joined a wider, more powerful river. She remembered Tyrel driving across a river. He had pointed out his mother's home sitting on a slight rise about a mile after crossing the bridge. She couldn't see the house but she was pretty sure she had spotted the highway.

Fixing her destination in her mind, she began running in that direction. She made one brief stop to have breakfast when a plump raccoon darted into the open just as she was exiting a creek. Once she had reached land below the cloud line, she noticed that her fur tended to stand on end from the high amount of static electricity in the air. The air was heavy with moisture, pointing to the possibility of a thunderstorm soon. She explored the forest, searching among the rocks for a place to ride out the storm. The sharp smell of ozone mixed with the mustiness of damp leaves. She looked to the sky, noticing that the thin wispy clouds of the morning had been replaced by heavy black thunderheads. Gusts of wind began flowing through the forest. Tall pines and cedars began to whip violently back and forth and the rain became imminent. As the first few drops began to fall, she stumbled across a small cave that a fox had used as a birthing den that spring. The kits were long gone, but the scent remained. As if they had been waiting for her to find a place of safety, the moment she was curled up inside, the dark clouds released a torrent of water upon the earth.

Chapter 6

Tyrel was watching a movie with his mother when someone started banging on her front door.

"Stay there," he said as Anola began to remove the blanket stretched over her legs, "I will see who it is." He wondered what the emergency was. It was nine in the morning and everyone knew his mother had been ill. No one would come for a social visit before noon. Something serious must have happened. He was surprised when Gwen's face popped into his mind. Today was her eighteenth birthday. He hoped nothing had happened to her. If she had been hurt, it would be logical to come here first, since he was the only licensed pilot in the area. Even knowing the possible bad outcomes from a females first shift, he had not seriously considered her being injured until he opened the door and found Gideon standing on the doorstep.

"Gideon, come in. What can I do for you."

"Thanks, I need to talk to you. Is there somewhere we can speak?"

Translation. I need to talk without your mother hearing me. " Sure. How about a cup of coffee and we can walk down by the catfish pond."

He poured them both a cup and the two men walked the short distance to the pond in the back yard. Tyrel say down at the stone picnic table and waited for Gideon to gather his thoughts. It was obvious something had him upset. He was reasonably certain it didn't require an emergency airlift but other than that he was stumped. After a few minutes, Gideon sat down and began to talk.

"I made a big mistake. Gambled when I was drunk. Lost a lot of money. More cash than I had available. Otto holds my IOU."

Tyrel nodded. This explained a lot of unanswered questions. Like why Otto had been seen around town with Gideon, and why rumors of his ascension to Alpha had been going around for months. "Okay. Just sell something and pay him off."

"I tried. He refused to allow me time to raise the money through conventional channels. The only asset I have that I can sell to raise the money quickly is Wolf Mountain."

"That complicates matters. It's one hell of a decision to make. I wouldn't want to be in your shoes. What has this got to do with me?"

"He offered me a way out. Otto returns the IOU and Gwen marries him. I signed the contract. I know it was stupid, I was desperate. I never expected them to meet. Then I found out that Otto had found Gwen. He pretended to be me, invited her to visit, even sent her a ticket in my name. I only found out when he told me you had picked her up in Atlanta and was on the way."

That explained why Gwen had no idea who Otto was. And why she had no idea what she was walking into. Everyone else on the mountain knew Otto was betrothed to Gideon's daughter. Otto would have made sure the rumor was spread as soon as the contract was signed. The smart thing for him to do would be to get in his truck, drive to the airport, and head back to Atlanta. He sighed. "Still no idea what this has to do with me,"

"Gwen disappeared. I'm certain Otto had nothing to do with it. I've got to give her credit, once she found out the farm truck would not start she wasted no time developing an alternative plan." He explained what had happened at the bar between Otto and his daughter, leaving out none of the details.

"So old Otto has a runaway bride, and everyone knows about it." Tyrel did not try and hide the pleasure that statement gave him. He could picture Gwen climbing out the window and down the oak tree. She had mentioned enjoying rock climbing as a hobby, that tree would have been a piece of cake. He was unsurprised to discover her father had no idea of her hobby. It was becoming evident her father knew very little about his daughter.

Gideon's hands were shaking as he struggled to get out the words. "We sent out trackers, searching the roads in all directions with no success. She left her purse and cell phone. I honestly thought Otto might have taken her. But after the fit he pitched when he found out she was gone; I don't think he had anything to do with her disappearance." He paused for a moment and sipped his coffee. "We finally found her trail leading down to the lake. That's where we lost her. She went into the water and no one has any idea where she came out. The damn rain ain't helping matters."

Tyrel nodded and sat quietly, going over what he had said. He knew Gwen was smart, there was no way she could handle a double engineering major without having a sharp mind. It was the other aspect he was worried about. "She's eighteen. She had no idea she was a shifter until you told her. By now she's already made the first change."

"We made sure she knew what to expect. And Mother talked to her about her first heat. I think that's what made her run, the idea of groveling before Otto and begging for his touch."

"So she could be a cougar. Do you know how hard it is to track a mountain lion? It's damn near impossible, and that's with a clear trail." The rain had been coming down for hours. Any scent would be long gone. It was going to be next to impossible to find her.

"That's why I came to you. You are the best tracker in the area. And after spending several hours with my daughter in the copter, I'm certain you know her scent better than anyone."

Tyrel shook his head sadly. "Trying to track her that was is impossible. Even if she managed her first shift, it only a matter of time before she goes into heat. That's going to attract any male cougar in the county. If she's even in the county. By now she could be anywhere. Where have they looked? Besides the roads and businesses?"

"A couple of Otto's men went toward the reservation. Otto's acting like a damn fool. He's called in all his chits and men have been coming in from out of town. He's got men staking out the resort and all the stores and the hotels over on the Bypass. Several shifted and started tracking her but lost her trail by the lake. One Sonovabitch laughed and said she probably drowned herself to keep from bonding with Otto."

Ty tried to picture the land around the lake. He was certain they were underestimating Gwen. She was smart enough to go into the lake to break the trail. She probably stayed in the water until she reached the creek. The question is whether she would follow the creek downstream and hope to find a street or if she went upstream. Most people would head downstream. Gwen was not most people. He knew she loved rock climbing. She would have headed for high ground. He looked across the field toward the river that flowed across the back section of his property. She was a smart woman. She had asked questions about the area as they drove in from the airport. He was certain she remembered the hairpin turn right before his mother's house. From the ridge above the lake, she would be able to see the road as it went into the switchback. He was willing to bet a week's salary she was heading that way. Not that he was going to mention that to her father.

"I'll shift and take a look around but it's a long shot. By now she could be in Cherokee. It would be simple to catch one of the tourist buses out of town, especially since she won't care where it's heading. It's doubtful I will cut her trail if Otto has had men looking for hours and had no luck. Just call mom and let me know if she's found. I'd hate for something to happen to her." He did his best to look doubtful but he wasn't sure if Gideon believed his excuses. Gideon was right, he did know her scent better than any of the others. And if she was out there he intended to find her. He remembered the lost, desperate appeal in her eyes when he left her at the cabin. A smart man would refuse to get involved. What was it about this girl that made all reason leave his mind?

Ty stood by the porch watching until Gideon's truck disappeared around the curve before going back into the house. "Mom. Do you know where my travel pack is?"

His mother was surprised. When Ty went hunting he didn't usually bother with his pack. He would shift in his room and shift back after he returned. He only carried his pack if he expected the need to shift while he was away from home. "It's in the closet on the shelf. I washed your clothes and repacked them. It should be ready to go."

Tyrel kissed her on top of her head. " Thanks. Gideons' daughter is missing. I promised him I would take a look." He knew his mother would not be fooled by his brief comment. She knew him well enough to know he would never do anything to help Otto.

He pulled the pack down, dropping it at his feet. Then he undressed before he shifted. Picking up the pack he padded into the kitchen.

His mother snapped the custom harness around his chest. " You've picked up some muscle. This is going to need adjusting before you wear it again."

"It's all your good cooking."

She opened the front door " Stay safe my son."

He rubbed his head against her leg then bounded out, running across the back pasture toward the ridgeline. In less than a minute he had disappeared into the forest.

Chapter 7

Topping the rise before the bar Otto was pleased to see the garish red neon sign advertising popular beer brands was not lit. The parking lot was full and many people were parking along the roadway by the time the council had set for the meeting arrived. His face broke into a wide, satisfied smirk. There would be more than enough voters at the meeting to certify his claim.

He stood in the door and allowed his vision to adjust to the dim lighting in the room before entering. The main room of the Sit-n-Sip was packed, there was a notice on the door saying the business was closed to the public and a guard was stationed by the entrance to ensure the meeting was not disturbed. So far, so good.

No one had been surprised when Otto requested a meeting of the community members. The news of his runaway bride had spread throughout the locals and most were secretly cheering the missing girl on. The fact that he had waited until Gideon was away from home to call the meeting was noted. Many were not sure they wanted to be involved with anything the Alpha of the Pride did not sanction.

Others felt it was past time Gideon stepped down and let a younger more progressive leader take over. Not that the three years age difference made Otto a more attractive candidate. A scattered few looked to Otto as a source of income and could care less if the more civic minded members of the community got upset.

Otto made his way to the front of the building and called out for attention. Around the room voices became silenced as everyone turned to listen to what he had to say. Some of the faces looked pleased. Others appeared cautious. A few were angry. But everyone wanted to hear him speak.

"As many of you know Gideon's daughter turned eighteen today. The chapel is decorated and everything was set for our bonding. Instead, when I went to have breakfast with my betrothed, I discover she has vanished. This is not a case of premarital jitters. She did not take her clothing, her cell phone, or her purse. Her father feels she had experienced her first change during the night and has run off out of fear. She may not understand how to change back to her human form. While I admit there is a possibility that Gwen had gone feral and is not able to shift back to human, my gut instinct is that someone had a hand in her disappearance. Someone who did not want her to go through the ceremony. "

Thomas Hicks, one of the older members of the pride decided he had heard enough. "Well, that all well and good. But if there's any chance she's run away, don't you think Gideon should be the one holding this meeting? He is the Prides Alpha."

For now. Otto glared his way before continuing. "Gideon has gone to Cherokee to talk to the tribal leaders. He wants to get ahead of the possibility she has gone rogue. You all remember the last time that happened."

Everyone did. Mikayla had been one of the most likable of the younger women on the mountain. She had been raised by her grandfather after her parents and grandmother were killed in a fire. The community had come together and built them a small cabin since the home was destroyed. Mikayla was five at the time.

By the time she was ten, nearby neighbors had noticed that Hezekiah had grown accustomed to treating her like a young boy instead of a young girl. Since her grandfather was too old to provide meat, she had taken it upon herself to ensure they did not go hungry. She set traps for small game and fished in the river. Because there was no money to purchase a gun or ammo, at thirteen she had fashioned a sturdy bow from cured beechwood and arrows from the reeds growing nearby. Tips for the arrows were fashioned from bits of metal she had scavenged. Within a year she had started supplying many of their neighbors with fresh meat, the funds she received enabled her to purchase many of the foods she could not catch or grow.

Mountain gossip suggested that during one of her hunting trips she had stumbled across a cave deep in the mountains. Inside was the dried out remains of several humans. They had been killed by some of the more aggressive cougars in years past. From the tooth marks on the bones, it was clear the bodies had been eaten, but the clothing and metal objects such as knives and coins were discarded as worthless. To Mikayla, they were a tradable product that would make life easier for her and her grandfather.

Mikayla had talked about her find with her grandfather, learning that in the past most of their people had considered humans a viable source of food.

Hezekiah told her it was only since the skinwalkers had begun to live among the humans in disguise that the Pride had outlawed the taking of humans for food.

Mikayla wasn't convinced that decision was a good one. She had brought up the subject in school and found out that many of her cousins felt humans were little better than any other meat animal. She thought about it and realized at home she had often enjoyed beef and chicken but had been told to avoid pork since it tasted so much like the flesh of men. She expressed her opinion to her friends, often stating she believed the pride was becoming too human. Everyone had considered her a typical rebellious teenager and laughed about it.

Otto knew the group was getting away from him so he started talking. "You all know the story of what happened to Mikayla. A twist of fate changed her life even further. Three days before her eighteenth birthday her grandfather was killed by a drunken driver while checking his mailbox. The police had shown up at the school to let her know about his death. Because Mikayla was so close to legal age, they decided to let her remain in the cabin on her own."

Morgan wondered what point he was trying t9 make. Mikayla had acted like any other adult. In the manner of the Pride, she had Hezekiah cremated the next day. Gideon had taken her to pick up the ashes. The next morning friends had gathered for the ceremony to say goodbye. No one had realized it was her birthday; especially not her eighteenth. While the mourners watched, Mikayla had walked to the back field, dumped the ashes into the wind, and cried. Then she began shifting. Most everyone was waiting by the house to give her private time. It was only when one of the young men mentioned seeing the mountain lion running toward the woods that anyone realized she was gone. She was never seen on Wolf Mountain after that day.

Three years later Gideon had been called to Cherokee to talk to the tribal police. They needed his help with a string of mysterious deaths inside the Qualla Boundary. Two were tourists, one was an older Tsalagi woman hanging clothes on the line. The mountain lion was feeding on her body when the old woman's grandson got off the school bus. He had seen the lion from the open back door and scared it off with a pellet rifle. Then he called 911. The tribe had tried tracking the cougar but it had evaded them. Fearing the big cat was a skinwalker, one of the tribal elders had sent for Gideon.

Gideon and the men of the pride had tracked the cougar to its lair. Inside the cave were the fresh bones of at least five human bodies. The pride had killed the man eater, only to stand in shock when it changed into a young woman as it died. One of the younger men recognized Mikayla. They had burned the body where it lay and sealed the cave.

Now Gideons' daughter was missing, ---on her eighteenth birthday.

Otto banged a chunk of wood to get everyone's attention. "We have been able to keep the Pride's existence a secret for many generations. Only those Tsalagi of the Wolf bloodline knows who really live on Wolf mountain. We can't take the chance that

Gwen has gone feral like Mikayla. We need to find her and if she can't change back, kill her."

"Don't you think you're rushing things? Maybe she took off because she didn't want to be forced into a bonding." Thomas Reeves asked. Gideon had mentioned he made a mistake waiting as long as he did to tell the girl about her bloodline. They had talked about it over dinner a few weeks earlier. He had been trying to think of an excuse to go and visit her and her mother.

Otto frowned at his comment. Thomas was often the voice of the more conservative members of the pride. It was no secret that he supported another Alpha as pride leader after Gideon. It was only that Alphas arrogance that kept him from stepping forward and staking his claim to the pride.

"I've heard enough of the bullshit." Morgan's voice rolled out to every shifter in the room. She had been sitting with her back to the wall at the rear of the building listening to Otto run his mouth for too long. All eyes were on her as she stood and began walking toward the door. When she got there she stopped and turned, "Answer me this. Is Otto worried about being rejected by the girl; or not being considered for Alpha without her at his side? It won't be long before Gideon steps down. Seems like you need to decide that question before you go running all over the mountain looking for someone who does not want to be found." As a roar of voices broke the silence, she shoved the young guard out of the way and walked out.

**

Finally, Gwen thought, I lost them. She stood still for a moment listening for the sounds of voices calling out in the woods below the rocks. She had been pleased to find out how easy it had been to change back into her human body. Once she changed it had been simple to climb up the sheer rock face. There was no way a cougar could climb it so no one was expecting her to be hiding there.

Gwen knew the only way a normal tracker could find her now was by chance. But if he cut her trail, a shifter tracking her by scent could find where she began her climb up the rock face no matter how hard she tried to hide it. Since most of them had grown up in the area, they were sure to know another way up the ridge. She needed to get some distance between them while she could. There was a creek flowing down the far side of the ridge. She had learned in Girl Scouts that no one could track her by scent in moving water. She intended to wade as long as she could before shifting back into a mountain lion. Even if they chanced upon her scent and followed it to the creek, they would have to take their time and cover both sides of the creek until they located the spot where she left the water. That's was going to take time.

She felt truly free for the first time in years. The cool water felt wonderful and she loved the way the sunlight felt on her bare skin. She had been surprised by how little being naked bothered her. She was carrying her pack on her head as she waded to prevent anything from getting it wet since she would need to shift back into human form once she reached the road. From the top of the ridge, she was certain she had spotted the sharp cutback near the house Tyrel had identified as his mother's. There was very little chance he was still around but that wasn't going to slow her down. Even if he had returned to Atlanta, Gwen felt confident she could find her way back to the main parkway. Then it would be simple to follow it back to civilization. It might take her a few days, but she had already discovered how easy it was to find food in cat form. The water was up to the middle of her chest and she was considering leaving the creek and shifting back to cougar when a familiar deep voice startled her.

"I got to give you credit, you were not the easiest person to find."

Gwen turned to look at Tyrel who was sitting on a boulder near the creek. She saw his face flush but he quickly covered it up with a wry grin. However, that did not stop his perusal of her naked body.

"It took you long enough. I figured you would have found me while I still up on the ridge."

He laughed. "Gideon didn't let me know you were missing until this morning. He's really worried about you. The rest of the pride is convinced you are heading toward Cherokee, but I had a feeling you were going high. Of course, no one else knew how much you like rock climbing." His eyes kept drifting down to her breasts, and he would jerk them back to her face. He was certain she had seen him looking, so he gave up fighting and let them travel slowly along her body. The lower half was under water but the part he could see was damn near perfect. Drops of water ran down her chest, dripping off the pert nipples. He was surprised by how much he wanted to lick the droplets away.

Gwen felt the weight of his eyes on her body and shivered as a rush of heat swept over her. She was surprised by the way her hair was standing on end. It was as if every atom on her body was alert and waiting. She looked around, suddenly overwhelmed by modesty, and moved the pack from her head, holding it in her arms in front of her breasts. "I need to come out of the water." She looked around but there was nothing nearby that offered a measure of privacy.

Ty somehow managed to give her the impression he was laughing. "Better come out and shift. We will make better time in cat form. "His voice seemed to come from a great distance and she realized he was no longer sitting on the rock.

"How do I hear you?" she called out as she waded toward shore.

"It will be easier once you shift. Everyone in the Pride can communicate this way. Unfortunately, that means anyone within range can hear us talking. One or two may have been smart enough to stake out my mother's house. So, hurry up and shift so we can put some distance between us."

Her expression changed from embarrassment to complete indifference as she waded toward the shore. The shift from human to cat became easier each time so it was a matter of seconds before she was padding softly around the big rock.

"You're such an ass." She wasn't sure what she was expecting when she rounded the corner. Maybe a light brown coat like her father. Instead, there was a dark brown, almost black cougar holding a pack in his mouth. A larger, more muscular cougar that looked deeply into her eyes. It had taken her years to build her wall so high no one would ever be able to hurt her again, not as a friend, not as a lover, no one. That wall fell in seconds. And in the far recesses of her mind she could have sworn she heard "Mate

Chapter 8

"Stay here. Let me scout around." Tyrel moved off into the underbrush, his dark mottled coat seamlessly blending with the shadows. One moment his muscular feline form was beside her, the next he was gone. Gwen flattened her body along the ground until only the tips of her ears were visible through the high grass. The two cougars had approached the airfield from downwind, hoping to catch the scent of anyone who might be watching his helicopter. When they arrived both were worn out from traveling across the terrain and panting heavily. For almost an hour they had lain in the deep grass without moving a muscle, concealed by the shadows and scrub brush. Ty had studied the buildings around his chopper, looking for any sign that someone had been there.

Everything looked exactly as it should appear. All the buildings were dark. The normal security lights were burning. It was a little strange to view the landing field it from a different perspective than the bench seat of his pickup truck as he pulled up to the building. The old ford truck was waiting at his mother's house. He knew she would ensure no one touched it while he was gone. He doubted anyone had found his spare key. Even if they checked through the chained down toolbox, it was doubtful anyone had thought to turn it upside down and look at the bottom. The magnetic key case had been one of his best purchases.

He doubted anyone would even bother dropping by her house to ask about his whereabouts. Otto knew his mother would not answer any questions. She hated Otto almost as much as Tyrel did. It was Otto's fault his father had died after a bar fight over in Gatlinburg. Otto had run into a couple of men from his former motorcycle club and his father had been shot during the ensuing brawl. He had lost consciousness while driving to the hospital and gone over the edge, falling several hundred feet into a deep ravine. His father's death had led to Gideon's rise to pride leader.

Tyrel often wondered if the fight had been faked as an excuse to take his father out. Otto had somehow managed to avoid any injury during the brawl. Witnesses said all four bikers were beating on his father when the shot rang out. No one was sure where the bullet came from. To avoid the police, the four bikers took off as soon as the bullet hit his father. No one remembered seeing a fifth man. Otto left the bar as soon as the bikers took off, leaving his father bleeding on the floor. Somehow he managed to struggle to his feet and stumble to his truck alone.

Tyrel never forgave him for leaving his father alone. He hoped it haunted Otto's dreams and kept him up at night. Otto knew Tyrel was an Alpha. It had to eat at him that Ty had a much stronger claim to clan leadership than Gideon. He simply had no urge to take control.

Otto might set a man to watch his mother's house but knew there was little chance Gwen would show up there. They would watch for his truck and follow it if it moved. There was likely a similar setup watching his chopper.

He rose from his stomach amongst the overgrown plants along the edge of the field and padded toward the back of the closest building, the only proof of his passage the faint outline of his body against the darker shadows. Unlike Gwen's lighter fur, his darker pelt blended perfectly. Ghostlike he flowed through the bramble, keeping his lean feline form low to the ground to prevent even an accidental glimpse of his movement. He slipped from building to building, searching for any sign that someone was watching for Gwen to appear.

There was just enough of a breeze to carry the fading traces of various shifters, making it difficult to figure out if anyone had been on the grounds searching for them. All of the scents were old. If anyone had been there, it had been several hours earlier.

Satisfied that they were alone for the moment, Tyrel returned to Gwen." It seems clear. Once we are dressed we will start working our way to the helicopter. As far as I can tell it hasn't been touched. I didn't find any trace of a stranger near the chopper."

"It's too bad we can't wait until we get in the helicopter to change back." There was a slight blurring before she rose from the ground and began dressing.

Ty crouched nearby as he shifted. Then he began removing his clothes from the pack. He tried not to look when Gwen shifted back to human but the temptation was overwhelming. She looked sexy as hell in the moonlight. It took all his will power to keep from rolling her over in the deep grass. He had no idea what it was about her that enticed him to push beyond the tentative friendship they had developed. It was almost as bad as puberty. He thanked his human side for his strong will, if Gwen had been in heat there was no way he could have stopped himself. As it was, he could barely keep his hands away.

Maybe just a taste… Before she realized what he had in mind, he pulled her into his arms, capturing her lips in a deep sensual kiss.

***

Tyrel's scent was overpowering Gwen's good sense. Her heart pounded in her chest and her body began to sweat. She could feel her skin growing warmer. She took a small step backward, then panicked when she felt the wall behind her. Tyrel's body stepped with hers, his kiss deepening, promising so much more. She fought hard to ignore the flood of emotions she felt whenever he was near. But, that kiss said so much more than friends. That kiss she would never be able to forget.

Finally, he stepped away and moved to the corner of the shed. If Gwen noticed his discomfort she didn't mention it.

They were almost to the helicopter when she saw Tyrel's head turn as he caught a glimpse of movement from the corner of his eye. He signaled for her to one eye on the edge of the opposite tree line as he urged her to hurry toward the helicopter. By the time they had reached the door and he was pushing her into the small cockpit area, she was certain someone was hiding in the woods on the other side of the field.

"Give me a minute. I need to get the key." She continued to watch the tree line as he shifted something heavy in the back of the cockpit. Seconds later he was back in the pilot's seat.

"Strap in. We may have to leave in a hurry."

He connected his seatbelt as she fumbled with the H-harness. She knew that once he switched on the engine it was going to take a minute or so to warm the motor. If there was anyone on the far side of the field, the sound of the engine would alert them. It would take them about the same length of time to cross the airfield as the engine took to warm up. It was going to be close.

***

Tyrel heard the crack of the rifle just as the bullet slammed into the back of his seat. "Shit! Get down."

Gwen let out a yelp of fear and ducked, hoping the shooter was too far away to hit his target. Not that it would prevent a lucky shot or a ricochet.

They were not worried about taking either of them alive. No longer concerned with noise, Tyrel pushed the control lever forward, throwing the motor wide open. Now was not the time to worry about possible wear on his engine. As soon as the rotors were spinning fast enough to left them off the ground, he took off, cursing the fact that he was unable to gain the height he wanted while trying to evade the gunshots. He gave up on altitude, shoving the control forward and skimming just above the treetops. At that low altitude, it was important to put as much distance as possible between the chopper and the gun. The helicopter was slowly gaining altitude but the mountains were gaining height even faster. He eased the stick backward an inch or so and felt better when the helicopter began to rise faster.

They were going to make it.

His relief turned to anger as he spotted the red extended cab Chevy pulling into the field, directly in the path of the fleeing chopper.

"Sonovabitch. That bastard was waiting on us. I should have killed Otto when I had the chance." Of course, Otto would have sent more than one man to the airfield.

Gwen heard the sharp retort of the repetitive shots just before she heard something strike metal near her head with a clang. Another bullet hit somewhere farther back. The helicopter's motor faltered then picked up speed again. Tyrel winced, not wanting to take a look. Sure enough, there was a thin stream of droplets coming from the bottom of the chopper. He was losing oil or fuel. Either one was a disaster. One way or the other, the chopper was going to come down long before they reached the next airfield.

"Cross your fingers. Transylvania airport is closest but there is no way Otto does not have that staked out. Same for Pickens's county, and Gatlinburg. They expect us to head south toward Georgia. They will head for Greenville, it's the closest big airport. We are going to have to swing around and try for Ashville. It's a long shot but the best chance we have."

"Won't that take us deeper into the mountains?"

"Yes. But if we do go down, I would prefer to land in an isolated area. A crash will make the news and I don't want our faces plastered all over the networks by the media." What he didn't mention was her physical condition. Her body was hyper-charged now. It was already beginning to affect him. He was disappointed she had not acknowledged him as her mate but that was not unusual. Until he marked her she may not realize they were mated. An unmated female was an attractive target. Within twenty-four hours her hormones would begin to radiate outward, attracting the attention of any unmated male within range. He wanted her, but not that way. He wanted her to choose him freely, not accept him while under the sway of runaway emotions.

In the distance he could see the first faint purples and pinks of sunrise peeking over the eastern mountains. It was less than an hour until dawn. Ty's eyes stayed locked on the gauges, wondering if more than one bullet had struck the chopper. There was a steady decline in the levels of both fuel and oil. Much as he hated flying so low in the darkness, he dropped the helicopter lower, weaving along just above the treetops through canyons and along steep mountainsides. The farther they flew the steeper and more rugged the terrain became until they were flying over land that very few men had ever walked. The helicopter had just passed Turnpike Creek just north of the Blue Ridge Parkway when the motor began to cut out. They would need to land now or they would go down the hard way.

He turned to Gwen. "Make sure your seatbelt is tight. I'm going to try and get us as close to the ground as possible. This landing is not going to be easy."

She looked around, seeing nothing but trees and rocks. "We are going to land on that?"

"No," he said as the engine stopped and the helicopter began to spiral down toward the ground. "We are going to crash on that."

Chapter 9

The phone began beeping, interrupting Otto's conversation. Not that the conversation had been going as he'd hoped. If anything, it was almost identical to the previous four. No sign of them. No one has heard of a helicopter coming in, especially a damaged one.

"Find more men," he snapped, before hitting the red end button and disconnecting the call.

"Talk," he growled as he answered the incoming call.

"Any luck?" Pete asked cautiously.

"Hell no. If anyone has seen them they are not talking. I've heard from Knoxville, Gatlinburg, Greenville, and every small independent airfield between here and Atlanta. It's like the chopper went into a cloud bank and disappeared."

"Maybe it did. Maybe Tyrel made a circle and went back to the same place he started from. Then he might have made his way back home and got his truck. He could be anywhere."

Otto's face paled. "Damn. That's one thing I didn't think of. He could have pulled a stunt like that.

It's something that twisted bastard would come up with. His father was devious like that."

"So what should I do? "Pete asked.

"Nothing. Keep Cherokee covered. That's still his best bet. He knows the tribal police would grant him sanctuary since no one is willing to break the covenant. If they make it onto the reservation, that's nothing we can do but wait them out. I will drive over to check out the landing field and see if the chopper is there. If it is, we can figure out what to do next." Otto sighed. They were running out of time. He needed to have the woman in his possession before she went into heat. If she did not bond with him then, it would be six months before he could force a bond. He was not sure if Gideon would live that long; pancreatic cancer was almost 90% terminal within six months of diagnosis. About a week before the fateful card game Otto had overheard a phone conversation he was having with his oncologist. The word malignant had jumped out. His mind had begun spinning his plan that night. It had cost him a chunk of money to find the doctor and get a copy of the medical report. The prognosis was not good. Stage four pancreatic cancer. No chance of treatment. Then he paid off the others in the game, claiming it was to teach Gideon a lesson.

Everything had gone as planned until the bitch had taken off, and with Tyrel Henderson of all people.

That had to have been Morgan's doing. Otto had to admit she was one cunning woman: easily smart enough to be the one pulling the strings.

He cranked his truck and pulled out into traffic, heading toward the small local airfield. Thinking about Morgan made him realize he might have a bigger problem than timing. Tyrel was an Alpha and would have been one of, if not the top contenders for the pride leadership. The only reason no one had considered him was because he'd left the area and moved to Atlanta. By now he had to have realized Gwen was coming into heat. Tyrel would be forced to make a decision; one he may not be willing to make.

His musing was interrupted by the phone again. He reached for his phone, fumbled it, and dropped it to the floorboard just as it began to ring again. Now who was calling? He had already heard from all his men, so it had to be someone else.

He pulled over and retrieved the phone, just as the ringing stopped. He didn't recognize the number. He thought about ignoring the call but gut instinct said he needed to return the call. Certain he was asking for more complications, he hit redial.

"Hello? "A stranger's voice…a woman?

"This is Otto. You called me?"

"Yes. This is Mary Judd. Over near Canton. My cousin is Robert Hicks. He mentioned you were hunting for a helicopter. We were fishing down on

Lake Logan last night and we saw one. It was flying low and smoking. The motor sounded bad. You could smell the oil burning. I think it may have crashed in the mountains right above the lake."

"Thank you for calling. I will have it checked out. You will hear from me." Otto's hands were shaking as he hung up the phone. He slammed his fist against the wheel, cursing loudly. Just as he feared, he had overlooked something important. He had been looking at this the wrong way. Tyrel hadn't headed toward a populated area. What if he was looking for seclusion? That area of North Carolina was about empty. There were parts of the range in that area so secluded no one living had set foot there. Tyrel could not have picked a better place to crash. The only question was why. Tyrel did not know the woman. Nor had he any intention of taking a mate. He could be looking for a place he could hide her away. All he had to do was keep her away from the Pride for the three or four days. That may be what Gideon asked him to do when they spoke.

He began calling in his men.

***

Gwen was out of her seatbelt and gathering her things before Tyrel said it was safe to do so. She loved horror movies and too many of them involved exploding aircraft after a crash landing.

Tyrel had brought the chopper down on a low saddleback ridge between two mountain peaks, higher than he preferred but in an area that would be difficult to reach. The rotor of the helicopter had clipped an outcropping of rock, throwing the chopper into a spin. It had bounced and thudded along the ground, sliding downward before the tail of the helicopter had struck something solid enough to forestall its plunge. Glass shattered. There was a screaming rip of metal followed by an assortment of tearing sounds from the passenger side of the helicopter.

Gwen remembered a faint sensation of pain as a black mist swirled before her eyes. Her subconscious mind disassociated her from what was happening as a hard bump of her arm against the side wall brought on a wave of agony.

A man's voice broke through the roaring in her ears, "Gwen! We need to keep moving. I know it hurts but we have to get out of here." Then an iron grip on her arm pulled her upward, toward the now shattered windshield of the helicopter.

Gwen did her best to shake the daze and do as he had directed. Tyrel had wrapped a muscular arm around her ribs, giving her some support to the trembling awkwardness of her legs. The wind whipped her hair into her face as she tried to stand. The sharp sting of rain against her face and the ominous rumble of thunder nearby added to the dangerous situation. They were high enough on the mountain to be inside the cloud layer. There was an ominous hint of electricity in the air. She wanted to collapse to the ground and cry but the rock hard arm around her waist would not allow it.

Ty was practically shouting as he sought to keep her moving. "We can't stop here. It's too dangerous. The metal of the helicopter will attract lightning and our wet bodies are perfect conductors. We have to move lower and get out of the cloud cover."

"I suppose there's some special cat god we are supposed to pray to."

"Yeah. Jesus."

Gwen mumbled a vicious curse under her breath but did not argue the wisdom of his statement. Not that it made walking any easier. Her right arm was throbbing and she could not lift it. At least the numbness was beginning to fade from her legs. Not that walking on the muddy slope was any easier. Ty prevented her from stopping until he spotted an overhang that offered some protection from the weather.

"Wait here. I need to go back to the chopper and get my emergency kit. I think your arm might be broken. I need to grab our packs, too. It shouldn't take too long."

She nodded, knowing he was only looking out for her. Was she being childish because she wanted to beg him not to leave her? Tyrel had made it clear that she would be a target for the lightning anywhere near the helicopter. That meant he was also a target. She struggled to get the words out before he walked away, "Can't it wait. The lightning …"

"No. All it takes is one random strike and the gas in the chopper will explode. Every minute we delay increases the chance it will happen before we get our things. I need to go now." He disappeared into the darkness without waiting for a reply.

Gwen watched until he disappeared into the darkness. Occasionally lightning lit up the area and she could see his shadowy form, first walking toward the crash site and then moving around inside the twisted wreckage. It was a miracle they had survived the crash. It was only because Tyrel had flown low atop the tree line that the crash had not been worse than it was. She just wished he would hurry.

She jumped when almost directly overhead thunder rolled and a flash of lightning cracked, followed by a boom as the helicopter exploded. Gwen tried to spot Ty but her vision was blurred from the tears. Had he still been inside the helicopter? She waited alone in the darkness.

Chapter 10

Gwen knelt in the darkness staring at the burning helicopter, watching for any sign of movement that might indicate that Tyrel had not been inside the chopper when it exploded. Rain continued to fall, sending rivulets of water down her face, making it impossible to tell she was crying. The wind whipped at her hair and the sting of chilled water against her cheeks increased. The weather was getting worse and they were high enough in the mountains to get hail, if not ice, even in early autumn. The ominous roll of thunder overhead was making her anxious and the nearby lighting strikes seemed to be increasing.

Gwen avoided looking at the flashes, hoping that her eyes would adjust as she tried to penetrate the oppressive gloom of the storm. Every time the lightning brightened the sky she hoped for a glimpse of Ty, but there were only the dying flames and the ghostly shimmer of metal reflected in the random electrical flashes.

Thunder boomed, followed by a crackling sound as lightning hit the metal of the helicopter again. Gwen flinched, only to shriek and jump again as a hand came down upon her shoulder in the darkness.

Expecting to find that Otto or one of his men had tracked her down, she jerked forward, twisting to see who was behind her. She was surprised to see Tyrel standing there.

"How did you get behind me?" She wanted to lean against his body and cry out her relief and thankfulness that he was alive but he was not going to give her that opportunity.

"That's not important. We need to move. The metal of the chopper is attracting lightning strikes. There's nothing to act as a ground in the area and your body makes a great target for the electricity."

Ty pulled her back to her feet, then waited as Gwen carefully shifted her injured arm, which he noticed was swollen and hot to the touch. She whimpered as the circulation returned to the blood starved tissue. He pulled her weight against him to help her to balance. Then helped her to hobble away from the wreckage, going first on the hill to prevent her from sliding down the muddy slope.

"Why are we moving higher into the storm?"

"We need to work our way through the ridge cut. The passage is not well traveled but there is a clear game trail for us to follow. The tracks will be washed out by the storm but they won't be hunting in human form. With luck, it may take them a day or two to locate the wreckage. We need to put as much ground between us and the trackers as possible.

Once we cross over to the other side we will leave the game trail and follow the ridgeline for a while. Tomorrow we will try to make our way to lower ground. They will expect us to continue to travel toward Ashville. I plan on heading south."

Gwen wasn't happy with his words but she knew she had to accept the truth of his answer. "Umm. Hate to mention this but I think my arm is broken." Her eyes bored into his as she mentally braced herself for the answer she knew was coming. He had made it clear that their lives were in danger, and not just from the lightning.

"Yeah, I saw that." He continued walking.

That's it? That's all the answer she was getting? "Don't you think I need to get to a hospital and get it set?" She did her best to hide the tremor in her voice.

"Don't worry about it. I will set it for you when we stop for the night."

"You will set it?" She knew he had been in the service. Maybe he had some medical training. He had mentioned needing to get his medical kit from the helicopter.

"Yeah. As soon as we find somewhere we can hold up for the night, you and I need to have a serious discussion. Remind me if I forget." He wondered what else she had not been told. Shifters never went to the hospital. Their blood was simply too different. The first laboratory tech that got ahold of their hyperactivated blood, would know they were not human. He could imagine the headlines now; Aliens live among us!

They would be hunted down and locked into military medical facilities for scientists to poke and prod under the guise of bettering humanity. There was no way in hell he was letting anyone get their hands on Gwen.

Just as Ty expected the game trail led across the cutback before becoming a winding switchback path down the opposite side of the mountain. They followed it for about twenty minutes watching for a possible way to leave the trail and parallel the mountain. Finally, his eyes settled on a limestone outcropping cutting through the budding trees, and he made up his mind. It wasn't perfect, but it offered the possibility of shelter, and that was about all he could expect at this point. Traversing the exposed shale surface was not going to be easy with Gwen's injured arm, but he was certain her rock climbing experience would enable her to manage the unstable crossing. There was a patch of heavy undergrowth they would need to transverse before reaching the shale slope that would have been easier in cat form, but there was no way a cat could cross that slide. Maybe it would keep them from being discovered while she rested and recovered.

"We are turning off here. There's no trail to follow, so be careful and make sure you have secure footing before you put your weight on it." After making sure she was following, he turned and started for the outcropping.

At first, Gwen had been surprised at how well she could see in the dark but she had now grown accustomed to her new eyesight and come to appreciate the accelerated night vision. After hours of using small saplings and exposed roots to help her climb, she finally reached the base of the shale slide. Testing the thin stone with her foot, she smiled, realizing it was embedded in the dirt better than she expected. As long as she placed her feet solidly before adding any weight, she was able to make her way across the slide with one hand. With Tyrel's help about an hour after leaving the trail, they reached the base of the limestone crag and ascended the rock formation. The jumbled rocks looked promising, there might be a natural cavity or a place to make a lean-to out of the weather.

Ty spotted the narrow opening before she did. "Wait here and let me check it out. This late in the season it's likely unoccupied but the weather may have driven something inside." He handed her his jeans and shifted.

Gwen was surprised at how quickly she had adjusted to the idea of him stripping down and changing shape. She had simply kept her eyes on the cave entrance instead of his body, pleased that he had been too busy undressing to scan her thoughts.

In seconds he was back, but he remained in Cougar form.

"Empty." He grabbed both packs and his boots, trusting her to carry his jeans and t-shirt into the cave.

Gwen was happy to crawl inside the small cave, content to be out of the rain for the first time since the crash hours earlier. A fox had used it as a birthing den in the past, there was a thick layer of dried leaves and grass atop the stone. Over the summer any biting insect had long since abandoned the bedding in search of a meal. The cave was not big enough for a fire, which was good since the only thing dry enough to burn was the bedding.

Gwen was tired and wet and irritable. Her teeth began to chatter. She was growing colder despite being inside the dry cave. She would feel better once she got the wet things off. Ty had dropped her pack next to his, so she began digging inside, searching for a dry shirt and jogging pants. While not the most attractive outfit, it would be the most comfortable to sleep in.

Not wanting to admit she needed help, Gwen attempted to remove her wet shirt. The arm of the shirt caught on her elbow, sending a sharp shooting pain radiating down her arm. Her eyes misted with tears. Gritting her teeth against the imminent discomfort she used her good hand to examine the area of pain. She was almost certain it was broken; it had begun to throb and stiffen up. There was no way she could do it without help.

Ty must have been watching her because he said, "let me take a look at your arm." His amber eyes held no hint of what was to come in their golden depths. There was a brief moment when he seemed out of focus, then he was kneeling next to her in the darkness.

Not even the pain could keep her mind off the fact that they were alone, in a cave and he was naked…and so damn sexy.

Tyrel carefully worked the wet shirt off her arm, forcing his eyes to remain on her face instead of the delicate lace brassiere that cupped her breasts. Thank goodness she was wearing one, it added a tentative shield of protection that forced him to keep his hands on her arm and away from her more attractive assets.

Gwen was affecting him in ways he never expected. It wasn't as if he never lacked female companionship, he spent his fair share of college mornings doing the walk of shame, or in his case the strut. Nothing serious, more a string of one night stands as he prowled the college bars along with the other members of his fraternity. After graduation he did three years in the Airforce, getting his pilot's license and saving up to but his helicopter. In the bars near the base there were plenty of single women hoping to hook up with a future pilot. There was something about Gwen that was different.

He wanted her as a mate and that had taken him by surprise. It wasn't that she was his version of feline perfection, he had always preferred curvier, full-busted women. But every time he thought about the way the water had dripped off her hair onto those perfect champagne glass breasts, he could feel his groin tighten. All it took was one stray thought and wham... he was hard as a rock. She didn't seem to be interested in him. His cougar was going to have to understand.

Gwen could feel his gently probing fingers move along the length of her forearm... his actions vaguely uncomfortable. Then he placed one hand on her shoulder and clamped the other around her wrist. "This is going to hurt," he warned, just before he jerked her lower arm, moving the bone back into position.

Although prepared, Gwen could not prevent herself from gasping out a sharp exclamation of pain. "Did you have to jerk so damn hard?"

"I warned you. Now hold still and let me check it."

"Fuck you! It hurts," she snapped, stating the obvious.

Ty ignored her and examined the break to make sure the bone was back in the proper location. Then he began to remove her boots.

"What are you doing?"

"Helping you undress. These are your favorite jeans and I would hate to see them ruined when you shift."

"When I shift? That's not gonna happen. I hurt too much to concentrate."

"And the pain is going to get worse unless you do. It's important that you shift now. The process will accelerate healing."

"Huh?" she was puzzled by his words.

"Shifting will heal the break. It won't be a hundred percent solid, but it will be a thousand times better than it is now. Now raise your ass and let me pull your jeans off."

Gwen used her good arm to brace against and lifted her hips off the ground, allowing Tyrel to slide her wet jeans off. When her underwear came off with her jeans she sighed, happy that his dark sight would not show the red flush that covered her almost naked body. The flush deepened when he reached behind her back and unsnapped her bra with a practiced twist of one hand.

Before he had a chance to comment, she concentrated on her cougar body and shifted. She was instantly warmer. And just as Ty had promised, her front leg easily supported her weight. Nor was there any pain. "You are right. It doesn't hurt anymore."

"It's still not back to normal, so you are not going to be walking around on it. Once you have warmed enough, switch back and get dressed."

Gwen noticed the distinct scent of fresh blood and nosed his shoulder. "Why didn't you mention you were hurt?" His composure was starting to irritate her. Did nothing faze him?

"Because it's just a small cut. It must have something in it, it didn't heal when I shifted. Once it's light enough, you can dig it out for me. There isn't much you can do until then." He opened his pack and pulled out a sweatshirt, noticing she had shifted back and was pulling on her stretch pants and a t-shirt. "We are out of the weather but it still gets cold overnight at this time of year. Try sleeping in this instead of that t-shirt."

She snuggled into the warm fleece, smiling at how loose the sweatshirt was on her slender body.

Tyrel pulled a small plastic wrapped package from his pocket, tore it open and shook out the contents. The thin plastic blanket was coated on one side with a metal substance that resembled aluminum foil, however, it was not hard or inflexible like the silvery metal. "Lie down and I will cover you up. You can use your pack as a pillow. "

She stretched out on the leaves beside him, enjoying the warmth from the blanket and his body, sighing in contentment as her body began to relax.

"Better," he asked.

"Hmm…" She inhaled deeply, enjoying the musky scent of his maleness along with the fresh clean aroma of the rain soaked earth. Gradually her breathing slowed and softened.

Groaning, Ty rolled over, or tried to anyway, since it was impossible with her head pillowed on his arm. How could she sleep so soundly after setting his soul on fire? The tiniest contact set his senses aflame. She had to have felt the same way. When the mate bond formed, it affected the entire body. After an hour he realized there was no way he was going to be able to fall asleep with her lying next to him. He carefully worked his arm out from under her head, smiling briefly when she mumbled 'no' in her sleep. He needed to put a bit of distance between them.

Tyrel sat and watched her sleeping for a moment more before moving to the front of the cave. Being so close to her and not having her acknowledge the mate bond was growing uncomfortable. He had heard of this happening. Usually, it was when the female was much younger than her intended mate and she had to mature. He had always assumed that meant a physical maturity. Now he wondered if there was some type of emotional growth involved in the process. Being half-human her blood quantum had never been tested. His nostrils flared as the scent of her unsated desire drifted his way. She was getting closer to heat and she still had not acknowledged him as her mate. Morgan would have discussed the basics with her because it was so close to her eighteenth birthday. What if the possibility of a mate bond had never come up in the conversation. She might not recognize what she was experiencing. He could smell her body changing, as the time of her heat was rapidly approaching. It would be so much easier if she understood the bond before the heat came on. He would have to take into consideration. It would be a lot easier if he hadn't kissed her. His imagination immediately kicked into overdrive and left him with one hell of an erection that refused to go away. Thinking about that lace bra didn't help. All he wanted to do was tongue her taut nipples to see if they tasted as good as they looked.

He sat at the mouth of the cave watching the last of the rain falling. Hours crept by, and the sky grew lighter. The section of the forest they had crashed in was not heavily traveled. There was no clear trail to the rock outcropping and the only way to easily reach it was from above. The overhang hid the mouth of the cave so no one would easily stumble upon the entrance. It was not a perfect location, but it was the best he was going to find under the circumstances. The rain would wash away all scent, it would be hard to discover where they had left the game trail. Otto's men's only hope would be to follow the game trail down the mountain hoping to catch them before they located a road or other sign of civilization.

Tyrel thought about the men he had seen drinking with Otto. Only one of the men gave him pause. Jasper was too honest to get involved with most of Otto's schemes, but the wily old shifter was one of the best trackers in the area. If he got within five miles of Gwen when she went into heat, he could track her across any terrain. If that time came, he would deal with it. Eventually, he crawled to the back of the cave, curled up beside her, one arm draped over her waist and fell into a fitful sleep.

Chapter 11

Exhaustion kept Gwen sound asleep until soft sunlight filtering into the cave awakened her to a beautiful morning. Sometime during the night, she had shifted position. Tyrel was lying beside her, stretched out on his back. Her head was snuggled into his shoulder, her arm rested across his chest and the rest of her length was curled up against the length of his amazingly muscular naked body. She wondered what her ultra-conservative mother would think about her waking up in the arms of a virtual stranger. At first she was conscious only of his irresistible presence, but gradually she began to relax and enjoy the warmth from his body. Her mind stopped dwelling on the idea of him being naked and began to wander into more alluring territory. She shifted her body to ease the twinge in her core but it didn't help. Not even a cold shower would put out this fire. Tyrel wanted her as much as she wanted him. She would have to be blind, deaf, and dumb to have missed the signs. But something was holding him back.

His lips were parted the tiniest bit and he was smiling in his sleep. It must have been a pleasant dream. Gwen wondered what he would think if she kissed him. Ty had seemed to enjoy the first kiss, which was evident by the way his body had reacted. It would have been impossible to hide that reaction.

Thinking about the way his cock had pressed against her made her shiver. His eyes opened slightly, giving him a sultry appeal that added to her discomfort. A soft moan escaped and she closed her eyes, trying to suppress the impulse to straddle his naked body.

Somehow he must have recognized her need. He looked into her eyes for a moment, then pulled her down into his arms without saying a word. She sighed, enjoying the feel of his arms around her, even though she would have preferred less clothing and more passion. Her nipples hardened and she arched her back, hoping he would take a hint.

Tyrel froze for a second as her body's reaction signaled more than he had expected. He wanted to tear the warm clothing away and show her exactly how he felt. But he knew that could ruin any chance of a voluntary bond. Instead, he pulled her onto his chest and kissed her. The kiss was soft, exploratory, almost too light. But her reaction was everything he hoped for.

Gwen's body tingled as his calloused fingers traced the curve of her face before he groaned and pulled her into a deeper kiss. His lips were firm and demanding, parting her lips with his tongue as he probed and teased. She met his lips eagerly, sucking and nibbling on his tongue as his lips caressed hers. She shivered as he tore his mouth away, moving to suck gently on her neck before his lips trailed feather-light kisses across her shoulders. Each kiss sent a tingle of pleasure from where they landed down the length of her body setting every nerve alight and centering somewhere deep inside her core. His hands slid down her back to her sides and she shivered as his fingers gently caressed her sides. It was like liquid fire as her body went up in flames. She burned on the inside and yearned for more. Then Tyrel stopped, pulling his mouth away slowly, and holding her out at arm's length.

"Damn, this is harder than I expected it to be."

Gwen's face must have reflected her disappointment because a soft groan escaped his lips. "You're not making this any easier."

"Show me where it says I have to do that in the cougar handbook," she replied, looking directly into his eyes. Even in the dimly lit cave, he could see how her pupils had dilated and darkened. Her breathing had quickened. She threaded her fingers around his head, using his hair to help as she pulled his mouth back to hers as a tingling warmth ran throughout his body.. Tyrel's eyes darkened and he groaned as he pulled her back into a deeper kiss. Then he pushed her away. "Mine" he whispered directly into her mind.

Gwen took that as a promise. She arched her body slightly, pressing her chest against his and shifting her hips.

Ty responded to her suggestive movement by rubbing her back, neck and shoulders, maintaining a slow, steady rhythm. Gradually his pattern widened, adding her waist and hips to his intoxicating touch. A forest fire began growing inside her. She tipped her head back and he responded by bringing his lips down to meet hers. The intimacy of being in his arms banished all sense of inhibition and she wrapped her arms around his neck, pulling him closer. Somehow everything he did felt right. The steady rhythm of his heart matched beats with hers and all sense of time disappeared. His kisses grew demanding as her mouth parted inviting his tongue to explore and tease. She raised her back, pressing her breasts against his hands. As of acknowledging some type of signal, he shifted her weight, sliding his hands under the edge of the sweatshirt.

Gwen gasped as his fingers touched her bare skin, sending flashes of pleasure along her body and deep into her core. Her nipples rubbed against the cotton of the shirt, and he groaned, before rolling it upward and pulling it over her head. Her pert breasts fit perfectly in the palms of his hands. In slow circles his fingers teased her nipples, rolling them between the side and stroking the tips. A soft moan escaped her lips, bringing on Ty's deeper groan in response before he rolled her onto her back. His hands began the same rhythmic rubbing along her body as his lips came down upon her breasts, gently suckling the pink nubs. The small flame in her veins engulfed her senses. She pressed harder, inviting him to suck and tease her more. She could feel the hard length of his swollen cock through the thin material of her jogging pants. Catlike, she managed to slide them off without breaking his rhythm. His hands immediately slipped down to her hips, stroking her ass with his thumbs, each circle growing closer to her moist core as her legs parted, inviting him onward.

The scent of his mates' arousal was driving Ty crazy, but he knew that the first time had to be completely her choice. He wanted nothing more than to sheathe his cock deep inside her and claim her as his own. His muscles tightened as he fought for control, wanting this to be perfect. Somehow he resisted the urge to rush, concentrating instead on the tiny pink bud between her legs. His finger slid between the silken folds, finding and caressing the sensitive button.

Gwen whined and jerked her hips upward, begging for more. His cock reacted with a twitch of its own and he could feel his cougar urging him to stake his claim. His lips claimed her mouth once more, each kiss demanding and receiving her complete submission. One finger slid deep inside, as his thumb stroked and tugged on her swollen clit. The enticing aroma taunted him for holding back. When Gwen's legs separated, inviting him and he slid down, eager to taste. His pleasure increased as her breaths became pants then gasps. The sound of her voice broke the spell.

"Ty, please. Now."

He moved upward with a groan positioning himself between her knees. Her hips gyrated slowly, and her legs parted, further inviting him in. His guttural response was more a growl than a moan as he slid the length of his cock once along the folds, then slick with her fluids he began a slow steady stroke, each time going slightly deeper until he was fully sheathed. "Mate." For a few seconds he lay there, content to feel her, then he once again began moving.

Gwen startled and froze for a second at the possessive sound of his mental voice before once again moving her hips, tightening her muscles. Ty seemed surprised by her actions but let her do what she liked. She wanted to tease him until he groaned out his desire, wanting to know that he needed her touch the same way that she needed his. Somehow things had changed, with that one word, "mine." It was as if a key had turned, opening him up to her and her to him. She reached back and cupped his cheeks, pulling him closer, urging him deeper. She needed to know he felt the same way she was feeling, this perfect almost desperate need to be part of him. Every kiss, every caress seemed so much more, a hidden promise that she had never felt before. There was something different in his touch, something intangible. She rocked her hips, lost completely in the rhythm of his movements, feeling the flames grow higher, and hotter with each stroke deep into her core.

Gradually her breathing increased, becoming deeper, in time with his breaths, until it seemed as if they became one. Bending slightly, he pulled the more sensitive right nipple deep into his mouth, sucking in time with the rhythm of his hips. Her muscles clenched and released, as she met his stroke for stroke. Like a cat, she bit down on his shoulder, and he jerked, only to have her begin to suck and nibble on his neck instead.

Tyrel knew she was close. Gwen was becoming erratic in her movements, unable to keep the perfect rhythm that had brought her there. Hell, it was driving him crazy, trying to maintain his humanity and balance out the pure animal lust flooding throughout his body. All he could do was concentrate on how good it felt being deep in her core and how great he wanted to make her feel. When she grabbed his ass wanting more, he gave it to her, sliding his ridge across that sensitive spot he had already recognized, thrusting faster and harder, until he felt her muscles clench and she exploded as wave after wave of ecstasy ran throughout her body. She clung to him as he followed her over the edge, spilling his seed deep inside her body. Gradually his movements slowed and stopped. Just before he collapsed bonelessly upon her body he heard her say "Mine."

His cougar roared.

Chapter 12

Tyrel laughed aloud. For someone who had grown up in the Smokey Mountains, he was surprised by how beautiful everything around him was. His head swiveled to the left and right as his eyes sought to take in every inch of the vibrant beauty around him. From the rock overhang on which he was standing could he see for miles in every direction. This deep into the forest meant the view covered see miles and miles of unmolested, lush, mountain terrain with very few trails to follow. To the north, a narrow game trail zigzagged through steep valley walls until it reached a more populated area just west of Ashville. To the south, Tyrel could make out a shallow creek winding through the foliage. Somewhere southeast of their location, that same creek joined a wider, more powerful river. He hated the idea of leaving their warm little nest and heading south but there would be too many eyes searching the area once word of the helicopter crash got out. It would be unrealistic to think no one had spotted the chopper and not realized it was in trouble. He was certain that the couple fishing on the lake had noticed them. If anyone came around asking he was certain they would remember.

He reached into his front pocket and found the metal pendant Gwen had left in his truck.

Gwendolyn. His Gwen. His mate. He was happy he had taken his time and not rushed into a relationship. He had wanted her to be aware the first time, to know it was him, and make a willing choice to accept him even though it had been dangerous. Making love that close to her first heat was risking the possibility of pushing her into a feral mindset, but it had been worth it.

He grinned, remembering the brief conversation that occurred when they awakened that morning. Gwen had so solemn, so serious when she asked her ridiculous question. "I hope you weren't too disappointed I wasn't a virgin."

He had been surprised to see tears welling in her eyes. "Don't tell anyone, but neither was I," he said.

"I know how important it is to traditional men. And I've discovered that cougars are really into tradition and family rules. I won't hold you to anything you might have said in the heat of the moment."

Tyrel chuckled at the oh so serious tone of her voice. "Too late. You can't back out now. You're mine." He grinned, showing that perfect little dimple on the right cheek as she paled. "Don't get all huffy over semantics. It was perfect. You are perfect. I can honestly say that you were worth waiting for." He kissed the tip of her nose.

"Harrumph…"

His golden eyes darkened, becoming more topaz than honey.

Gwen could tell he had not liked her answer. Had he changed his mind? For a moment she felt weak and nauseated. A surge of acid twisted her gut as she fought back the urge to hurl. "Don't be angry, I tried."

"Angry?" His voice deepened to a growl, "What makes you think I would ever be disappointed by anything you do."

She hesitated, struggling to put her thoughts into words, then gave up. "Looks like you got the short end of the stick in the draw. The pale skinny half breed."

He started laughing. "Have you noticed a lot of blondes around here? Almost everyone in town has some native blood. When our people floated to shore the local natives took care of us. No one judged. This was many hundreds of years ago. Since then humanity and the Maahzini have often mixed blood."

Gwen had nodded at his words but he was sure her mind was running through every possible scenario and assuming all the worst ones were her future. He had already discovered the strong outer image concealed a soft, sensitive inside.

The best thing he could do for Gwen would be to put as many miles as possible between her and Otto. The mate bond had been created but it had not been sealed and witnessed. Without the Prides acknowledgment, it could cause problems once they returned to Wolf Mountain. He was worried about Gwen not understanding the commitment of a mate bond. Her body recognized him as her mate, but there was something in her mind that prevented her from opening herself completely to their bond. Hopefully, she would begin to trust him and accept the connection they had. Once she accepted it, the Pride would honor her decision, and perform the ceremony.

Otto was going to be a problem. He would never accept the idea of them being a mated pair. Since it was a lifetime bond, Tyrel knew Otto would need to kill him if he hoped to force Gwen to form a new bond. She was his ticket to the Pride, and everything he always wanted, money, power, and a sense of belonging. Otto hadn't always been a rogue. At some point in the past, his Pride had cast him out. Ty often wondered what the burly, middle-aged shifter had done that was so heinous, that his pride would drive him away from his family…forever. Once they were safe, he needed to hire an investigator to get to the bottom of the mystery. The sun was setting over the western ridge. He hated to do it but it was time to wake Gwen.

***

Gwen stretched and opened her eyes. Her body ached from sleeping on the ground and muscles she had never used before were sore and tender. She was surprised by her sudden brush with modesty as she tugged on her t-shirt and underwear before looking around for her stretch pants. Somehow they had ended up too near the mouth of the cave and gotten wet from the rain. She pulled her last pair of jeans out of her pack and rolled up her damp ones, sliding them inside along with her bra and wet tee. They had dried out considerably since their soaking the night before, but they all felt damp to her. The faint acrid scent of mildew irritated her sensitive nose. The t-shirt might have to be trashed and the jeans would need washing and deodorizing before she could wear them again.

Once Gwen decided she was decently covered and her hair was brushed, she joined Tyrel at the front of the cave. She had to give him credit, other than his jesting pout when he saw she was dressed he did not make any comment or offend her sense of modesty. He had smiled warmly, then pointed out a fawn playing in a small meadow near its mother. The doe was grazing at the edge of the clearing below the rocks, keeping one eye on her fawn and somehow watching out for predators at the same time. She would not have been so calm if she knew two cougars were looking down at them.

The morning air was cool but many times warmer than yesterday's rain. She would have been content to sit there for hours. Instead, Tyrel mentioned the unhealed cut on his shoulder.

"I would like you to take a look. I must have gotten a sliver of glass or a piece of metal in it when the helicopter exploded. That's when the cut occurred."

"Do you want me to look now?"

His gaze moved lazily across her body. Then he grinned rakishly and she blushed." I want you to do that and much more. But that's going to have to wait for a more opportune time. I guess I will have to be satisfied with you examining the cut." He opened a pocketknife and passed it to her. "You may have to use my knife to clean away any debris."

She examined the razor sharp five-inch Gerber blade. "Too bad it's not one of those red ones with all the contraptions."

"Nope, I actually use mine to work. The Swiss sell their knives primarily to boy scouts, bored housewives, and end of time preppers. They would not last a week under real workplace conditions."

"Then by all means let's get right to it," she replied dryly.

Gwen giggled like a little girl at the peeved expression that crossed his face at her words. As she began to clean the cut, she talked, "You will soon come to realize I'm prone to foot-in-mouth disease. It always happens at the worst possible moments. Contrary to the old saying, what you say can hurt you. I'm living proof of that."

Ty thought it was pointless to get into an argument about something so trivial, even though she had inadvertently started the conversation with her terse response. He turned his body so she could examine the wound, accepting her awkward apology without comment. The gentle probing of her fingers made him wince when she touched the offending object, but he remained silent.

"Ouch. Sorry, didn't mean to hurt you. There's a small piece of metal here. Tweezers would have helped but I should be able to work it out with the tip of the blade."

Ty smiled. As she worked his eyes strayed to her neck, and the soft pulse at the vee below her collarbone. The memory of his lips pressed against her throat and other spots on her body drew an immediate reaction. He shifted his weight, taking pressure off his growing cock. There was no time for that right now. Even spending the night and sleeping had been taking a dangerous chance. Several seconds had passed before he realized Gwen had finished removing the sliver of metal and was waiting for him to put his t-shirt back on. Caught staring, he had the decency to look guilty.

"Should I bandage it before you dress?"

"Not necessary. I'm going to undress and shift as soon as we reach level ground. You might as well shinny out of your jeans now and put them in your pack. We will make better time that way."

***

The paired mountain lions studied the terrain below them, trying to decide what would be the best course of travel from this point on. For several hours they had been working their way south from the area of the wreckage, gradually moving downward toward the stream Tyrel had spotted from the cave. The heavy storm last night had unleashed torrents of rain. The ground was oversaturated and the runoff now poured down the steep mountainsides. Puddles of water expanded and joined together, forming shallow ponds that often blocked the game trail they were following. The banks of the once peaceful stream could only handle a limited amount of water before it overflowed. Eventually, the turbulent creek pushed back, forcing the runoff up the steep slopes back onto the surrounding land.

Gwen's eyes swept the meadow, searching for a safer route than wading through the shallow water. The water level had risen steadily and was still rising.

Even mature trees looked like scrub brushes, some barely peeking their heads above the surface.

It was approaching dusk as the exhausted pair reached the banks of the swollen creek. There was nothing peaceful or tranquil about the angry, mud-stained cauldron that churned below them. The water flowed with such ferocity it sounded like a train approaching.

Tyrel tried to picture where they were, but most of the nearby landmarks were hidden by water. He knew they were in friendly territory; however, the leader of the neighboring Pride was the type of leader that often took the path of least resistance. He would not prevent them from traveling through the area, however, it was doubtful he would hide them from Otto or his men. But Gwen needed a safe place to rest. His Uncles cabin was the only place he could think of. After traveling all day, between all the detours and forced turn backs from the flooding, they had only managed to cover about ten miles of actual ground. Ty's immediate qualm was the water level. It was so high any experienced tracker would be aware of the limited crossing points, and head straight to the bridge.

"At least we don't have to worry about going thirsty," Gwen quipped lightly as she paced alongside the rushing water.

Tyrel cut his eyes Gwen's way at her weak attempt at humor. "No but finding something to eat may be harder than usual. Anything with common sense has headed for higher ground. We might get lucky and spot a raccoon in a tree." By his estimate, the creek they were following would soon join the South Fork Mill River. Once they reached the river and turned downstream, they should reach the Wolf Ford bridge in about an hour. The bridge was the only way across the river for miles. His family had homes on this side of the bridge and would shelter them for the night. Herman wasn't a member of the Wolf Mountain Pride and would have no compunction about screwing over Otto or her father. Otto would bother them while they were sheltering with his family. They could wash clothes, take a hot shower, and rest. The problem would come once they crossed the river into the Pisgah National Forest. Once they set foot on the other side, they could not claim the protection of the clan.

Tyrel took one last look at the flooded landscape below, then turned his gaze to the crest of the mountain nearby. It was so far away, but it was the only logical direction anyone tracking them would travel. Once the wreckage was discovered, Otto would send his men out in all four directions in hopes of cutting their trail. One or two were smart enough to realize with the water levels so high, he would need to find a way across the river. The older ones might remember his uncle.

Ty sighed. He would deal with that problem when it occurred. For now, he needed to get his new mate to safety before she went into heat. That time was growing closer and becoming more and more uncertain as the hours passed. He was worried. Now that they were both in their cat forms it was easy for him to identify the chemical changes that were occurring in her body. In a matter of hours her hyperexcited hormones would balloon and she would experience heat for the first time. He went over the terrain between them and his helicopter. Several dirt roads led into and out of the area. They could make it but it was going to be close. All it would take is one or two detours to leave them inside Wolf Mountain territory when her time came. Then all bets were off.

Somehow he had to ensure he was the only male around when her time came. The cards had fallen in their favor since they began heading toward the airport but that was going to change soon. In the four days since Gwen's birthday, he had come to realize she was his true lifemate. He was not going to share her and he wasn't sure she understood what would happen if other male cougars were around. "Remind me after we settle down for the night that you and I need to have a serious discussion."

"We are alone now? What is it?"

"It can wait. It's not much further now. I know you are tired and hungry. We will sleep in a real bed tonight and worry about the rest tomorrow."

Gwen nosed him and gave his face one tired lick, then followed him as he moved off into the underbrush.

***

Smoke! Adrenaline gushed through Ty's veins, giving him the strength to move forward. Gwen's paws were raw and bleeding, and his were beginning to swell. Long underused muscles sent bursts of pain along aching limbs with each step. After hours of brutal walking, the two mountain lions crested the small summit and stood in the open clearing while Tyrel searched for the source of the smoke.

Less than a quarter of a mile away stood a small collection of frame houses and log cabins. Wispy gray smoke lazily rolled from several of the cabin's chimneys. If he'd had the energy, he would have jumped for joy. Instead, he waited on Gwen to join him on the knoll.

"Is that it?" Her warm brown eyes were lit by a renewed spirit as she gazed down at the small community. The evening sunlight gave a picturesque quality to the setting, making it appear like something from a fairytale. Not a single cloud marred the scene, every storm cloud from the previous night had disappeared. A hawk was soaring lazily across the sky, searching for his dinner. Two children played basketball, while watched over by a large grey dog. Nothing about the scene below made her uncomfortable.

"Yes. We should arrive a little after dark. The river is still up pretty high but the area near the bridge is banked. I doubt they have experienced any flooding. More than likely no one but my family will be around."

He began moving steadily toward the distant houses, following one of the creeks that fed into the river. Gwen hadn't noticed him walking away. When she realized he was leaving, she took off after him, not realizing her speed was too fast for the water saturated ground. As she approached him, she tried to slow down but the mud under her paws shifted, throwing her completely off balance. She made a desperate effort to regain her footing, but her body hit the slick ground with a loud smack. The mud under her body convulsed and she began sliding forward and downward, like a water park thrill ride. Tyrel made a desperate lunge to save her but he was too late. She hit the swift water of the creek and was immediately swept away.

Tyrel wasted no time thinking. He broke into a run along the riverbank, trying to get ahead of her flailing body. His eyes scanned the terrain, searching for anything that might stop her forward motion. About a hundred feet beyond him, a shattered oak tree lay partially buried by the floodwaters. Realizing this might be his only opportunity to save her he ran for the tree. With only seconds to spare he managed to shift back into human form and lay face down on the tree. As her body was swept under the tree, he dug his fingers into her fur and held on.

Panic had replaced all hope in her eyes, as she struggled to keep her head above the water.

"Gwen! I have you. You need to stop fighting me!"

"Don't let me go. Please!" Gwen was practically screaming in his mind. Tyrel had his hands locked around her neck but had no idea how he was going to get her out of the water. At least she was not flailing around any longer. The water was cold. It had to be draining her strength. He looked but there was nothing he could use to pull her out. Then he felt the touch of a familiar mind.

"Hang on Ty. I have a rope in my pack. I will be right back."

"Hear that baby? Help is here. He has a rope. We are going to get you out. Try and stay calm."

"I'm trying I'm just so tired." Gwen's thoughts were faint and fading. Ty knew she was losing consciousness. They needed to get her out and warmed up soon, or she might not make it.

"I'm back. I'm going to have to lie down atop you boy. Don't get no funny ideas. Lying on your naked ass ain't my idea of a good night either."

Gwen made a half-hearted attempt to laugh at the picture that formed in her mind. She had no idea who the naked old man was lying atop her mate. It could have been Otto and she wouldn't have cared. He had a rope and was trying to maneuver it under her body. Once he had a knot tied, he pulled it forward, directly behind her front legs and pulled it tight.

"Gwen. Listen to me. He has the rope wrapped around a tree up on the bank. You can't go any further. But I need to let you go and help him pull you to the shore."

"No! don't let me go!" She panicked as Ty released his grip and began thrashing around again.

"You are making this harder," Ty snarled directly into her mind. "Stop fighting us."

Gwen took a deep breath and tried not to struggle against the pull of the rope. Now that she could feel her body moving toward the shore she began to help, paddling desperately. In less than a minute they were pulling her waterlogged form onto dry land. Her last memory was hearing the stranger say, "Oh shit. Otto is going to have a conniption."

Then everything faded to black.

Chapter 13

The click of the door latching behind him as Tyrel left the room startled Gwen out of a wonderful dream. Her eyelids fluttered, and she opened her eyes, disappointed that she could not remember what she had been dreaming about. She was certain it had been a good dream, she felt warm and relaxed both inside and out. Of course, some of that might be because of the thick quilt she lay under. She yawned and stretched, breathing in the refreshing scent of freshly laundered linens. The bed was just soft enough, and the brushed cotton sheets felt wonderful against her bare skin. She could smell Tyrel's heady masculine scent on the pillow next to hers, and smiled, knowing he had slept beside her. That had been something she feared; that he would no longer want her once they left the forest.

She wondered where he was now?

Someone had washed and dried her clothing. It was folded neatly, lying on a chair next to the bed. She quickly donned her undies, then slipped into her favorite Eagles t-shirt. Her mother had passed it on to her on her sixteenth birthday, after introducing her to Joe Walsh, whom she knew from her band groupie days. The t-shirt was older than she was, but it was still in great shape. She debated between her favorite jeans and the ones she had been wearing, which she now considered her lucky jeans. Then slipped back into her favs. Meeting new people was never easy for her, and this was Ty's family. She needed all the confidence boosters she could get.

She had vague memories of being carried through the woods to the cabin, then several men's voices, and an older woman. Tyrel must have showered her off, she could smell the apple strawberry scent of the shampoo in her hair. With her hair brushed free of any sleep snarls and lying in an auburn sheen around her shoulders and down her back, she felt reasonably presentable. Spotting her boots sitting on the floor beside the chair, she stopped and considered putting them on, then decided barefoot would do for now. After pasting a wide grin on her face, she headed toward the sounds of voices in hopes of finding Tyrel there.

The main room of the cabin functioned as a great room, with both living, dining, and kitchen all in one area. Tyrel was leaning against the kitchen counter talking with two older men when she walked into the room. Even from across the room she could tell that whatever the two men were saying was making Tyrel noticeably upset. She stood at the bottom of the steps and waited for them to notice her.

Tyrel's grin when he saw her standing there widened her already beaming smile. "Gwen! We were just talking about you."

Suddenly overcome by nerves, Gwen was tempted to turn and run back upstairs, but she knew that would not endear her to Tyrel's relatives. After several deep breaths, she walked over to Ty and stood rooted by his side, acting as if meeting a family of cougar shapeshifters was an everyday occurrence.

It turned out that Tyrel's uncle Herman knew her father and had even met her mother once. "You took you looks from her, thank goodness. Not that your father is a bad looking man, she's just one hell of a good looking woman. We never did see what she saw in him, but everyone knew what he saw in her."

Gwen nodded; thankful his statement had not required an answer. Her eyes noticed the clock on the microwave, surprised to discover it was already a quarter afternoon. Ty had let her sleep in, and she had not thought about the fact that they needed to find a safe place to wait out her heat.

Tyrel must have caught a glimpse of her thoughts because he answered her unspoken question. "We are staying here. Uncle Herman is going to lock us in the bedroom upstairs and ensure no one disturbs us." Then he realized he had not even introduced her to either man.

"I guess the stress is getting to me. Gwen, this is my mother's older brother, Herman Wolf." He pointed to the tall, heavily built man sitting at the head of the table. Like Ty, his native blood was easy to see. He could have been anywhere from fifty to eighty, and like Ty's mother, he had wrinkle-free skin and dark hair, with a sprinkle of silver strands.

Herman stood and pulled her into his arms. "Welcome to the family."

Gwen realized he meant every word. "Thank you. This means a lot to me."

Jasper continued to sip at his coffee, waiting politely for Ty to introduce them. Ty did not make him wait long. "Gwen, this is Jasper Judd. He is the reason you are sitting here safe and dry."

Jasper stood and offered her his hand. "I wouldn't say I was the only reason. Ty had his fingers locked in a death grip on fur. I'd be willing to bet he would not have let go until the creek went back to normal. It might not have been the most comfortable night but you would have made it. I've seen a lot of mate bonds in my time, but yours is one of the strongest I have ever experienced."

Gwen wasn't sure if he expected her to reply to his comment, or how she should reply if she did.

"You two can consider this your honeymoon. Lay around and get to know each other. We might be getting older but my shotgun knows no age.

Between the gun, our teeth and our claws, no one will disturb you…even if one of them gets lucky and stumbles across the cabin."

"Yeah, it's doubtful that's going to happen," Jasper added. "Last time I laid eyes on Otto he was sending his men north toward Highway 40 and east toward Ashville. He said he was gonna head back toward your mother's place in case you doubled back that way. I suspect none of them even thought about your uncle."

Herman nodded. "You're probably right. But you found them. That means there is always a possibly one of the others might." His voice grew slightly louder. "Don't matter. The bond is already made. Like it or not, Tyrel and Gwen are mated for life. Otto's gonna need to find another way to worm himself into the hierarchy of the Pride.

Gwen had been looking around the cabin as the men talked. Though the vintage structure had more than basic creature comforts, the lack of advanced modern technology was evident. There was an old fashioned dial face telephone hooked to a landline. She knew the television in the room worked and she was willing to bet the computer in the corner could be hooked to the internet via a modem, but it was nothing compared to what she had in the city. She had left her cell phone behind, so there was no way to check for a signal. She yawned, wondering what she felt so sleepy after spending so much time in bed.

Ty noticed the yawn. His eyes narrowed darkly. "You seem tired. Why don't you go back upstairs and lie down? I will be right behind you. I just need to talk to Herman and Jasper a moment.

Gwen smiled and nodded, before saying her goodbyes and heading back up to their room to lie down.

As Gwen walked back to her room, Ty's uncle stood, "I could use some help bringing in some firewood. Electric heat doesn't warm the cabin the way the wood stove does. There's still a bit of a chill in the air after all that rain. My arthritis can't handle the change in the weather like it used to."

"Surely most of the rain has fallen?" Tyrel asked, sounding slightly puzzled.

Herman replied, "It has, but all of the tributaries that feed into the Mill River haven't dumped into the main branch yet. This is just the south fork. When the high waters from all those little streams feed into the river..."

"Sounds like it's about time to close the bridge," Jasper added.

"I'm going to walk down and check the levels in a few minutes. It's possible the water might come over the bridge. Might be the best thing that could happen."

Ty spotted the full wood rack as soon as he walked outside. There was already a basket full next to the woodstove, so it was obvious his uncle did not need wood for a fire. He waited, knowing he would find out the real reason soon enough.

His uncle collapsed in the rocker as soon as the door closed behind them. "Damn son, hope you been taking your vitamins."

Jasper grinned. "Makes me wish I were thirty years younger. I might be tempted to give you a fight for that one myself."

Herman laughed. "If it weren't so damn serious it would be funny. Problem is, within the next twenty-four hours every unmated male within ten miles or so whose balls have dropped, is going to start showing up. One or two of them may be cocky enough to try and take you on. Think you are up to it?"

Tyrel allowed the tiniest smirk to cross his face before he got it back under control. "I'm willing to die trying. It's doubtful any of them are."

"That's true. Still might be a good idea to fix it so no one can get across the bridge for a while. Gonna need your help though. These old bones ain't got the strength they used to have." Herman pushed his body back to his feet, then stretched. "Need to stop by Reuben's place on the way to the river. His boys ain't gonna be very happy when they get off work this evening but Reuben can handle them. He mentioned they were sniffin' around this morning and acting antsy. As soon as they took off for town, he dropped by. Lois was teasing him about his feeling frisky this morning."

Tyrel grinned. His uncle Herman had been about eight when Reuben and Lois bonded. The boys were change of life twins that neither had expected. Now in their mid-twenties, the brothers were more into video games and bar hopping over in Gatlinburg than settling down, especially with a woman who had already formed a life bond, no matter how tempting she was. Since it was Friday anyway, the idea of spending the weekend in town wouldn't bother them a bit, especially when they found out Tyrel was the one footing the hotel bill. The upcoming cost of the weekend made him wince a bit but it was a small price to pay to avoid having to whup them both. One at a time was no problem but the twins never did anything alone. That thought made him laugh as he remembered the girl that discovered the hard way that one twin had a small mole on his ass cheek and the other one didn't. She had not considered their little game funny in any way. Nor had her big brother, the tribes' former golden glove champion and current Army Ranger. Tyrel had witnessed firsthand how hard it was for one man to whup the twins. Knowing it could be done didn't make him want to attempt it. It was a whole lot easier to pay the expenses of a wild weekend in Gatlinburg.

Herman led then to the center of the bridge over the river. Then he pointed to a series of twenty-four metal panels. Each heavy mesh wire panel was about three feet wide and four feet long and set into slots along a six-inch wide metal beam. He turned to Tyrel, "You get to do the hard part. Jasper and I will pick up this side and move it onto the panel behind it. You have to lift your side up on its end and flip it toward us. But be careful, if it falls in the river, guess who is going to pay to have it brought back up."

"Wait a minute. That's all fine and dandy on the first three, but what about the next row? That beam ain't but six inches wide." Ty's eyes kept cutting between the narrow beam and the water rushing beneath the bridge.

Herman let him sweat for a moment before the two old men broke into roars of laughter. "You look like some just slipped in through the back door and made off with your bride." He pointed to a metal swing arm on a pole just before the panels. "Get into this safety harness just in case you lose your balance. The rope will keep you from being swept downstream. All you have to do is hook that chain onto that arm there and swing it over to the first panel. You need to lift the panel a bit so you can slip the hook around the slot in the metal frame. Once you are ready, I will pick it up and swing it over here."

Working together the job was finished in less than an hour. Reuben walked over to see how the job was going and congratulated Tyrel on his new bride. When they were about finished he asked Jasper if was interested in going for a run to check the backwoods water levels. The two men left together, leaving Tyrel and Herman to finish up. Once they finished, Tyrel studied the eighteen-foot gap, mentally gauging whether the distance would be enough.

Herman must have heard the same question before because he answered it before Ty spoke. "I have seen one make it. The other five fell into the river. And that was on a clear summer day when the water level was down and the stream was flowing slowly along. One might be crazy enough to try. Hope he's a good swimmer because the nearest low bank is a good mile downstream. That warning is printed on the sign on that post over there. Along with a warning that four men have drowned trying to make the jump and that no one has succeeded."

"I thought you said one had made it."

"One has, but they won't know that. He's out in the woods with Reuben right now. Worse fight Reuben ever had was when he had to ensure his claim to Lois. Jasper had been crazy about her since primary school. Both men were laid up for weeks after that fight. Crazy thing, they been thick as thieves ever since. Jasper ended up mated to Libby, one of Reuben's cousins from Virginia. Met her at the binding celebration."

He picked up his tool bag and they walked back toward the cabin. "Got a bottle of Champagne in a cabinet in the kitchen. You can take it with you when you go up. Might want to pack a few snacks too. It's gonna be a long weekend and you will need to keep up your strength." He grinned wryly. "Just in case…"

Chapter 14

Soft beams of early morning sunlight coaxed Gwen from a restful sleep. She yawned and stretched, before turning over and kissing the forehead of the man sleeping next to her. Ty's eyes cracked for a second before he relaxed back into sleep. She smiled. It had been one hell of a night, one that she hoped she would never need to discuss with her father… or anyone else.

Just thinking about it made her core tingle and her hips twitch. She had not been a virgin since she was a senior in high school. She had wondered why she had never really enjoyed sex the way her friends described it. No rockets, no fireworks at all. It was all right but nothing special.

When Ty had made love to her in the cave, she was certain there could nothing better. She was wrong. Nothing she experienced before could have prepared her for the wild, unbridled lust she has experienced with Tyrel. That wasn't making love. That was fucking. Now she understood the difference. Her body was hypersensitive to the smallest touch. She had an itch and he had to scratch it, over and over and over again. She had been insatiable, greedily taking everything he could give and still wanting more. It was only after her body had become so exhausted she could not continue that she had finally collapsed into a light fitful sleep.

Gwen stretched again, languidly, like a house cat, and realized she wasn't the least bit sore. This surprised her because she had used muscles she was certain she had never used before. Even the bite marks on her shoulder had healed. Ty had mentioned that no other male would bother her now that she was his mate. The mark on her neck and shoulder would warn the away. After a quick shower she headed downstairs to look for something to eat. She was ravenous.

She dug through the refrigerator, looking for something, a fresh kill would be fantastic. She would settle for rare. Hell, raw sounded great right now. After digging through every drawer, she had to accept that there was no uncooked meat. She had to be satisfied with half a ham and a chunk of cheddar cheese. She thought about making a sandwich, then decided to hell with the bread. She wanted meat, and the cheese didn't sound bad.

After placing them on the table she decided to be polite and slice off a section to eat, instead of simply taking a bite. There had to be a knife in a drawer somewhere. Gwen turned away from the counter and reached for a drawer. Then she screamed.

***

Oh shit. Trouble's coming." Jasper pointed to the men milling along the road leading to the gap in the bridge. Earlier a couple of the men had tried to make the jump and failed. They had hoped watching their friends get swept downstream by the rushing water would discourage them. However, the overwhelming primeval urge to procreate with the female in heat must have been stronger than either man anticipated.

There were now at least thirty men on the far shore. Normally, they would have been tearing each other apart, while trying to whittle down the number of competitors. Instead, they were trying to figure out a way across the gap. One had used a car to increase the range of his leap, running at the vehicle, and pushing off from the top. This had helped his range, but not his targeting. He had slammed into one of the stone columns and dropped insentient into the water. There was very little chance he survived.

It was the second day of Gwen's heat cycle. Last night one of the men had traveled cross country and come in from the back of the property. It had have taken him all night and most of the day to get there. He had been so exhausted; the two older men had no problem rounding him up. They had slipped him into a life jacket and dropped him into the river, figuring he was smart enough to survive the trip downstream.

He had.

Today he was back, and he brought a bigger, much smarter friend. They came pulling up in a Fire Engine, complete with an extension ladder. The new man backed the truck up to the gap, blocking the road. Then he walked around to the back and extended the ladder across the opening. It took him five minutes to reach the far side.

It would not take much longer for the men on the far side to realize he was across and follow him. Herman could see one of the watchers climbing up the front of the truck.

"What the hell is that girl? Even bonded she is throwing off enough pheromones to attract every unmated man in fifty miles."

"I have no idea," Jasper replied. "It's tugging at me and I've been mated over forty years. What do we do?"

"Pray? Run? Grab a gun? Your guess is as good as mine. If I had an alternative way of dealing with this situation, I wouldn't be standing here pissing in my boots."

"Well, we need to figure out something soon. There's another standing on this side of the bridge and it doesn't look like he's the type to share."

"He human or cat?" Once again Herman cursed his fading eyesight, he could not see the two men from where he was standing.

"Both still human. Oowee…one man just cold-cocked the hell out of the second. He must have been hiding something because number two went out like a light. Number one is dragging him toward the river. I guess he intends to dump him over the side."

"Unconscious and no life jacket? The man has no chance." Herman was worried. If Tyrel got wind of the other men within such a short distance to his new mate, he was liable to lose it. They were safer facing the river than the young, newly mated mountain lion.

"I wish I recognized him. But they are both strangers. Saw a couple of the boys from Wolf Mountain, but no idea what pack these two are in."

"There's two more on the ladder and but I'm keeping an eye on the big mutha. It won't be long before they are all across. We need to head for my cabin while we still have a chance to get there."

"Sounds good to me. Maybe they will take each other out before the rest arrive." Jasper shifted the shotgun to his shoulder and began backing toward the cabin. Herman was right behind him.

"Not the kind of luck I've been having lately, "Herman said.

"Your luck? With my fucking luck Tyrel's little fishies are not swimming. We may be facing another full day of this shit."

"At least the twins are out of town. They are just crazy enough to take on their cousin. We would end up burying at least one of them."

"True. Let's concentrate on staying alive long enough to celebrate the binding next week. The rest can wait."

***

The crash of the window frame breaking as the man's body was forcibly ejected from the cabin was the only warning the two older men had that there was trouble at the cabin.

Before the man hit the ground, Tyrel was through the window and charging his way. "Don't ever touch my mate again," he snarled as he reached for the young man lying on the ground.

Uncle Herman winced as the first blow landed on the strange man's chin, spinning him around. Before the young man had a chance to get his balance, Tyrel hit him again, a strong uppercut into his abdomen, followed by two jabs to his chest and shoulder. He collapsed to the ground. Ty seemed to ride the body downward, landing atop his chest and shoulders, pinning him to the ground. He pulled his arm back to deliver the Coupe de Grau, then realized the young man was already unconscious.

"Well fuck. Looks like we don't need to warn you that they are breaking through."

"No shit. Do something with this. I see another problem coming." Tyrel dropped the man's body back to the mud and began walking toward the group of men down by the bridge. Two of the men were already circling each other, watching for an opening. He could see blood on the ground. This wasn't the first fight, and from the looks of things, it wasn't going to be the last one. Most of the men looked like low-level betas, nothing worth worrying about. They would pace around and snarl at each other but none of them were of any consequence.

Herman motioned for Jasper to grab the young man's legs as he grabbed his arms by the shoulders.

One man caught Tyrel's attention. He was a burly, heavily muscled man with a full beard and long hair pulled back into a tail similar to Tyrel's. Full sleeve tattoos covered both arms and from the pattern, it would probably continue across his chest and back. There was only one Pride that had an Alpha that fit that description. Calder... Damn. The ex-marine was the son of the Morning Star Prides leader. Taking him out might not be as easy as the first scuffle.

He watched Calder as he walked up to the gap in the bridge, ignoring the majority of the men, and called out to the other alpha.

"I got someone that belongs to your Pride. Gonna hook him to the swivel and send him back to you. Might want to get him to shift soon."

"Tyrel. Fancy running into you here. I heard you had moved down to Atlanta." He kept his eyes on Herman and Jasper as they hooked the man to the chain and swung him over the gap. Two of the men helped unhook him and carried him to a blue pickup. They rolled him into the bed, shut the tailgate and then took off, scattering gravel in their rush to get the injured man to a healer. Calder switched his attention back to Tyrel.

Ty wasn't going to let him have any kind of advantage. "My work takes me there but my home is still on Wolf Mountain. Why are you here, disturbing my bonding time with my mate?"

"Mate? There's been no notice of your binding. When did you take a mate?"

"Less than a week ago. It was unexpected but sometimes that's how it happens."

A skinny boy with a face only a blind woman could love spoke up, "She ain't your mate. Otto has a bounty out on you and the woman. She was promised to him by her father."

"Fuck Otto. Gwen is my mate. Until death. Old Otto is going to have to deal with the fact that he will never have her."

Calder shoved the red haired boy out of the way. "Didn't know anything about Otto. I came to claim her as my own. Her scent does not show a mate bond. Are you sure it's not just wishful thinking?"

"Certain enough to die to keep her. Are you willing to risk death for someone you have never met?"

"For a chance to be the alpha of Wolf Creek Pride. Hell yeah. Besides, you walked away. I won't. " He began unbuttoning his shirt. Tyrel watched as he dropped the plaid flannel to the ground. When he reached for his belt, Tyrel did the same, keeping one eye on Calder and the other on the small group of men. Unlike Calder, he wasn't wearing boots or a shirt, just the jeans he had pulled on to walk down to the kitchen. Allowing Calder to undress was a courtesy. It was also a sign that Tyrel wasn't afraid of him. Calder knew this already. He had been in a few dustups with Tyrel over the years. Neither had suffered major injuries. But none of the fights had ever happened during a heat-induced fervor.

Calder kept talking. "Gideon is getting old. Rumor has it Otto is already planning a takeover. That's not going to happen. I've already dumped two of his minions into the river. There's plenty of room for you to join them." He glanced up toward the cabin where Gwen had just walked out into the porch. She was standing alone, looking down toward the river.

"Damn. I see why you are so set on keeping her for your own. One fine looking piece of ass. Too bad you haven't been able to stake your claim. You shootin' blanks?"

"Naw, I heard you got that covered. My mate won't be leaving me for another man. The bond is secure. Gwen is mine and no one is going to come between us."

Carder didn't bother with the fire truck ladder. Instead, he looped the belt over the hook on the swivel, got a running start toward the gap, and swung across. Herman and Jasper watched in shock as he easily made the crossing.

"Damn, why didn't either of us think about that?"

"Just getting old I guess."

Calder walked slowly toward Tyrel without saying a word. Ty expected him to circle or make some type of feint to feel him out before the fight began. The enlarged pupils and slight tensing of the other man's body was the only warning Tyrel had. He stood perfectly still and watched the blow coming, knowing there was no time to avoid it. Calder slammed his ham sized fist into his face and he went flying backward into one of the cement columns. Before he regained his feet, Calder drove a knee into his right kidney. Ty fought the wave of dizziness that swept across his body from the pain. Calder had him in a chokehold, trying to squeeze hard enough to knock him unconscious.

With a tremendous effort, Tyrel managed to drive both thumbs into the hollow of his challenger's throat, leaving him gasping and choking. He immediately slammed his forehead into Calder's face, lacerating the skin under the left eye. The blow loosened Calder's grip on his chest and Tyrel was able to wrench his arms free. He heaved and threw the bigger man backward before he had a chance to recover from the effects of Tyrel's blow.

Ty stood for a second, getting his balance, then made a feint toward Calder's kidney. Calder dropped his hands to protect his left side. This gave Tyrel the opening he needed. He stepped in and snapped his fist into his opponents' jaw, a hard jarring blow that made his arm spasm from the impact. Calder went sprawling on the ground in a heap.

Tyrel hoped the bigger man would stay down, acknowledging his right to Gwen. No such luck.

Calder had no intention of losing or giving up as long as there was breath left in his lungs. He waited until Ty's eyes were sweeping the faces of the other men, then ran at him from behind. His rush and grapple drove them both to the ground, where they rolled over and over, both men punching and swinging wildly as each fought for an advantage. When they hit a parapet and finally stopped rolling, Tyrel's fingers were locked in an iron grip about the bull neck of the bigger man. Calder's face reddened and his breathing slowed before his eyes rolled back in his head.

Not wanting to kill him, but still wary, Tyrel stepped away. He moved cautiously, never relaxing his defense until he was out of reach. Then he turned and snarled at the other men, who began moving about uneasily. A couple had already begun the trip back across the ladder.

"Leave Now or die. Gwen is mine." His comment was matched by the roar of an angry mountain lion behind him. The instinct for self-preservation took over and he turned, not an instant too soon, to meet the beast's challenge. Both feet left the ground and he shifted in the air, his muscular body morphing from human to cougar before his paws struck the packed earth road.

Hate crazed yellow-green eyes flared; drool dripping from bloody jowls, and great fangs gaped to seize and destroy him. The blood madness was upon Calder. The beast wanted his blood and his death. Tyrel fought to maintain his humanity.

The two big cats bit and clawed and scratched and struck, and all the while they kept up the most frightful chorus of growls and yowls and roars. In five minutes they were both torn and bleeding. Clawing and kicking desperately against the stomach of his opponent, Ty tore open the tender flesh above his groin.

The cougar yowled in pain and Ty managed to pull his damaged leg away from the injured cat. Scarlet stream of fresh blood stained the fur on both faces and legs bright crimson.

Herman could see that one of the cougars was limping on a savaged leg. The other cat's stomach was torn open and his intestines were hanging outside its body. He had no idea if it was Tyrel or Calder who limped away. Jasper passed him a rifle and they both began running toward the injured men.

By the time they reached them, both men had morphed back into their dominant human form. Herman was relieved to see Tyrel was the one with the injured leg, but he was still worried about the other alpha. There was a lot of blood in the dirt and he wasn't making any effort to rise from the ground. Now that he was close enough, he recognized the heir to the Morning Star pride. This was bad…really bad.

Herman knelt beside the bloody body and carefully examined the wound. Tyrel's claws had ripped his stomach open. Even with the shifters' hyperactive healing factors, he wasn't certain Calder would survive.

"Jasper go get doc. Grab the stretcher while you are there. Tell her it's bad. Run."

Jasper didn't waste time replying.

Herman took off his shirt and used it to apply pressure to the wound. Tyrel turned a bit green but he remained standing nearby, keeping one eye on the men gathered on the far side of the bridge.

Calder's eyes were wild, and rolling, he knew he was dying and he realized his time was limited. He gestured for Ty to come closer. "Tyrel listen to me. This is important. There must be peace between our people. Tell my father this, 'The road less taken is not always the safest.' He will know by my words that no revenge is needed."

"You can tell him yourself when you see him. Doc is coming. She will sew you up and have you back on your feet in no time." Tyrel hoped his doubts didn't show on his face. He was about to say something when he felt a hand on his shoulder. He jerked around, knocking Gwen off her feet. Her hands grasped desperately for anything to stop her from falling, but they found nothing. With a thud, she landed on her hands and knees in the bloody mud.

"What are you doing down here. It's dangerous," he snarled. Then he realized she was no longer throwing off pheromones. Her heat was over.

"I was worried about you. I had to make sure you were alright." She reached for his hand and he helped her to her feet.

Calder looked up into her eyes and smiled. "Yeah, she would have been worth it. I see what you mean now. She is your life mate. Lucky sonovabitch."

Doc had approached without the two men seeing her. "I'm happy for you, too. Now move out of my way and let me get this IV going. Seconds later she added, "Say goodnight Calder. You are about to go to sleep."

"Goodnig…."

Chapter 15

Jasper looked at the pale man sleeping in Doc's hospital bed and wondered if he had a snowball's chance in hell of surviving. He had never seen anyone recover from a stomach injury as bad as the young man's. He had assisted Doc as she carefully moved every damaged section of Calder's mangled intestines back into their normal position. His liver had been shredded but the liver healed faster than any other organ. He had lost a spleen but that wasn't needed anyway. Doc had meticulously reattached every artery and vein, doing her best to reconnect all of the damaged muscle. She had given him two units of plasma before she managed to stop the bleeding. Now all they could do is wait and hope his natural healing factors were enough to pull him through, or at least get him healthy enough to shift again.

A knock at the door made him jump. Jasper had not realized how tense he was. No one would be able to approach the Docs clinic without passing Herman or Tyrel. That meant they had a right to be there. He rose from the chair and opened the door.

It was Calder's father.

The usually robust and vivacious man looked twenty years older. He stood staring down at his son, tears streaming down his face. Calder was his only child. His wife had died in childbirth and the boy had become the center of his life. It was no surprise he was devastated.

Caleb nodded to Jasper, and then turned to Doc and asked, "What are your thoughts?"

"His heart rate is good, strong pulse in all of his limbs, abdomen sounds are normal," she replied.

"But what are your thoughts? I don't want a patronizing answer like you would give to a teenage mother with a sick baby. I want the truth."

She sighed in frustration, "He's strong and that helps. Tyrel kept his temper and that surprised me, considering his mate was standing on the porch watching the entire time. There is no way to know more without imaging and I do not have a CT scanner."

"Damn it, Lois, that doesn't fucking tell me anything. Is my son going to live?"

Doc shot him a reproachful glance but she let the less than socially correct language go. She would probably be worse if something like this had happened to one of her twins. "I don't know. The fact that he's still alive is in his favor. I was able to stop the bleeding and piece all the damage back together. I've kept him sedated as much as possible. The less he moves the better the chances he will heal completely. The next twenty-four hours are key. I think if he makes it through the night, he will pull through. But that's just my opinion. It's not a guarantee."

Caleb collapsed in the chair next to the bed. He reached for Calder's hand and held it for a few minutes.

Jasper gestured toward the door and Doc nodded. He would head over to Herman's cabin and let Tyrell know Caleb was in town. Then he was going to leave this side of the bridge and head back toward Wolf Mountain. One of the first things he needed to do was to let Tyrel's mother know what was going on. He also needed to talk to Gideon. Otto was going to be a problem and Gideon would need all the time he had to come up with a way to get out of the contract. Gwen was now bonded to Tyrel but Otto was an idiot. He might try to force the mating, believing she would accept him if Ty were no longer interested in damaged goods. He was underestimating the mate bond they had formed. If Otto touched Gwen, Ty would not only blame Otto; he would probably kill him.

Doc decided Caleb had visited long enough and his father would have to understand she needed to check his vitals and reflexes.

"Go sit in the chair by the door. That way you can see everything I am doing. I will let you know if I need help with anything."

Caleb watched her as she worked her way from Calder's head down to his feet, checking for muscle tone and blood circulation. Every so often she would stop and scribble notes on a clipboard. When the exam was finished, she leaned over and asked, "Calder? Can you hear me?"

"Yes." His voice was raw and little more than a whisper but he had answered.

Tears flowed down Caleb's face. Before Doc had a chance to ask him anything else, his father had crossed the room and was now back in the chair by the bed. "Son? I'm here son. You need to rest and heal. I will be beside you the entire time."

Calder squeezed his father's hand. "I know dad. I'm just tired." He lay quietly for a moment and then asked, "How's Ty?"

"I don't know. I haven't thought to ask. Doc? How is Tyrel?"

She thought about how much she could say to Caleb without irritating an already raw wound. "The gash on his leg will take a while to heal. He may have a limp for a while, but he should heal with no long term damage. He's resting at his uncles."

"That great," Calder said. "I can't believe I let myself get that crazy. If it had been anyone other than Tyrel, I would have been dumped in the river along with the other refuse."

A strained look passed across his father's face but he did not comment. "The only thing you need to worry about is getting well. Rest now. I will be here when you wake up."

He nodded at Doc and she injected a painkiller into his I.V. line. Calder was asleep before he realized what she had done.

Caleb stood. "I want to thank you for all you have done. If you had not taken care of my son, he would have died. He's all I have. My life…" He broke down, crying heavily into his hands.

Doc patted him on the shoulder for a moment. Then she gathered her things and walked out, closing the cabin door behind her.

She had a lot on her mind, not the least of which was getting Tyrel back on his feet. The two newly mated young folk needed to complete the binding ceremony so that Gwen was accepted as a member of the Pride. At this time, no one in the village had any idea of what was happening over on Wolf Mountain. They were certain of one thing; if Otto was involved in it, they knew it wasn't good for Gwen or Tyrel. The waters of the river rose fast and fell the same way. By morning they should be able to replace the metal plates and open the bridge across the river. After that, there was no way to know how long they had before Otto and his crew showed up. Tyrel was not in shape to fight another challenge. Not that anyone expected Otto to make a formal claim. He was the backstabbing from the shadows type. Tyrel needed to get Gwen to the Council and get her admitted to the Pride now before it was too late.

Instead of going back inside and resting Doc headed for Herman's cabin. There was a lot they needed to discuss. And some of it Tyrel was not going to want to hear.

Chapter 16

"What can we expect once we arrive at your mother's? Is she going to give us hell about the way we handled things?"

Gwen was glad she had used a strong antiperspirant after she showered; she could only imagine how her shirt would look without it. Her hands were cold and clammy. She had already soaked a handkerchief and was digging through Herman's glove box looking for a spare.

Gwen had no idea why she was so nervous. She had never had a problem meeting the parents of any of her earlier boyfriends. Of course, this was a bit different. If her mother-in-law hated her, she was stuck with her for life. Well, until the end of her mother in laws life anyway.

Tyrel laughed at her anxiety and squeezed her hand. "My mother is going to adore you. She has been hinting about not having grandchildren for the last three years. You could be completely human, bald, and ten years older than me and she would not care as long as you could get pregnant."

"That makes me feel special." The cynicism was evident in her tone.

"You need to relax. My mother is not a dragon. Cougars are very maternal. She would sooner throw me out than the mother of her future grandchild."

"But what if Otto is waiting for us to arrive?"

"The likelihood of him being anywhere close to my mother's property is so small, it's not worth mentioning. Him coming onto her property would give her a legal right to blow his head off. He knows it. He might send one of his followers over to the main road watch for us but he won't come near the house."

"So it should be quiet?"

Herman laughed. "Quiet is not the word that comes to mind. You are the talk of the town. Once word gets out that you and Tyrel are a mated pair, you won't be able to go anywhere without people staring. Cats are naturally curious, and Cougars are just big cats. Don't be surprised if people find an excuse to pop in to check out the mysterious stranger who left Otto at the altar and bonded with the black sheep of the Pride. You are an enigma wrapped in a mystery in a town full of gossipy men and women. They are gonna love you."

Gwen didn't care to meet a lot of strangers, but it sounded like a moot point. The two men seemed to take it for granted that there will be a steady flow of visitors. "When do you think they will start showing up?"

Ty laughed. "Start? According to my mother, at least half the Pride has already found a reason to drop by. She is hoping that they will respect our time of bonding and give us a little breathing room. But don't count on it.

***

Otto slammed his fist down on the table hard enough to make the salt and pepper shakers jump. "There's got to be a way to get this bond annulled."

"I'm not sure how they do it out west, but around here, once a mated pair is bonded, there is nothing you can do to break the bond." Pete signaled for the waitress to refill his coffee cup. Otto loved to meet at the tiny twenty-four-hour restaurant on the parkway leading into Murphy. For some reason, he thought it was safer to talk in a public location than in the privacy of his own home. Otto could have picked a place closer to home but this place was only a few blocks from his warehouse. Even though it was late in the tourist season, the traffic was still heavy enough that many of the seasonal restaurants and shops remained open.

It wasn't as if he had anything better to do anyway. A confirmed bachelor, Pete was married to his job. There had been gossip around the building supply warehouse he managed a few years ago, rumors about a possible relationship between Pete and another employee. When Michael had been killed in an automobile accident, Pete had taken to drinking, often sitting alone in his office with a bottle after hours. No one felt comfortable enough to ask, so it had remained an unanswered workplace rumor. The truth was Otto didn't figure it was his business and could care less as long as it didn't affect his life. As long as Pete showed up when he called, he was willing to accept him as he was.

Pete finished the last bite of his pie and stood up to leave, picking up the check for both men off the table. "The bond is for life. There's not a lot you can about that."

Otto's face broke into a smug smirk. "True. But some people live longer than others".

***

Of course, it would start raining again.

Gwen sighed, mentally cursing the inclement weather just before Herman pulled into Ty's mothers' driveway.

Tyrel looked at the dark clouds and declared no possibility of it stopping anytime soon. He handed Gwen his jacket to put over her head. "Just make a run for the porch, I will be right behind you."

Gwen nodded and dashed for the front door. In her haste, the toe of her boot caught the metal edge of the door's threshold stripping, sending her flailing. Her hands grasped desperately for anything to stop her from falling, but they found nothing.

With a thud, she landed on her hands and knees on an enormous bearskin rug. The bear's glass eyes reflected her flaming face, adding to her humiliation.

Tyrel's laughter broke the shocked silence, "You would not believe how tempting that looks, but since this is my mother's home, it will have to wait for another day."

"Haw, haw. Very funny. " Gwen's knees stung but that was nothing compared to her damaged dignity. For a moment she considered climbing back to her knees and crawling quietly out the door to avoid the humiliation. However, she reasoned being seen creeping out the door by your new mother-in-law would be more embarrassing than the actual fall. She struggled back to her feet and tried to rearrange her disheveled clothing.

"Are you alright?" Herman asked.

"I'm fine, thank you," she muttered.

Tyrel cleared his throat to keep from laughing again, "Good; because my mother loves that stupid rug and she would probably want to get rid of it if it hurt you."

Tyrel's joking banter eased her humiliation and Gwen decided to let it go. Ty helped her to her feet just as a graceful Native American woman walked into the room from the kitchen. Though Ty's mother had to be in her early fifties, the radiant smile made her look almost a decade younger. Her perfect skin showed only the finest of laugh lines around her sherry brown eyes and her once jet black hair was now lightly frosted with silver. An image of Tyrel at a similar age flashed before her eyes and she smiled briefly, surprised that such a thought would ever cross her mind. The bond made her feel like she had known him forever, but a baby had never crossed her mind.

Anola was still smiling as she wrapped Gwen into her arms. "Welcome to the family. You don't know how happy I am to meet you. I was beginning to believe Tyrel would never find his mate."

Gwen blushed. She had no idea what she expected, but this warm and welcoming greeting had never made the list." Thank you. It was a bit unexpected for me, too. A lot of things have happened to me in such a short amount of time. Finding Tyrel is one of the happier experiences."

Anola gestured to the couch while settling down in an overstuffed chair sitting catty-corner to the fireplace. "Would you like something to drink? Tea or Lemonade? A coke? Ty, go get her something." She turned to Gwen, "It has to be hard to accept some of the things that have been thrust upon you without warning. Tyrel said you grew up in a completely human family in a large metropolitan area."

"Everything is new and filled with things to learn. Life in New Orleans was certainly different from living in the mountains. But there is so much here to see. The forest is full of unique plants and animals. About the only animals, we ever saw outside of the zoo was an occasional alligator that wandered into the city from the swamp."

"I think you will like spending more time in the woods. There is so much to discover, not just about the land, but about you. All your senses are amplified, but I guess you have already noticed that."

Gwen blushed, remembering how she had spent almost an hour listening to the wildlife down by the pond. Before transitioning she had never noticed the whispery buzz of a dragonfly's wings, or how many different croaks a bullfrog made. One new experience was how different things smelled. Meat that was only a day or two old now made her queasy. She wanted it rare, freshly killed, and still warm and bleeding if possible. She had always hated liver but now, she would fight you for it. And she had started wearing sunglasses during the day. This had surprised her since even in Nolo, she had avoided them whenever possible. Her eyes were extremely sensitive to light, but she could see much better. "It has its moments."

"You might like another benefit since I know all young women worry about their weight. You will never see a fat cougar. Some of the males get a beer belly now and then, but once they shift they go back to their initial form. Your DNA imprint holds true no matter how much you eat."

"I noticed that some of the cat forms are more muscular than others. Is this normal?"

It depends on the shape they were in when they shifted for the first time. Males transition two years earlier than females. I think they need the extra time to mature. Now that you have come of age, you will start developing muscle that normal humans would die for."

This surprised her. " I hate to ask, but what the hell happened to Otto?"

Anola laughed. "Otto is a pig. He drinks so much his body is fighting against him. He never shifts, preferring to use a gun and his minions to provide his meat." She stopped talking and a funny look passed over her face for a few seconds, then it was replaced by a smile. "Otto is in for quite a few surprises now that Tyrel has taken a mate. My son will be spending more time at home, at least until the baby is weaned."

"Baby?" Gwen felt her jaw hit the floor. Baby! I can't be pregnant. Can I? Oh, my Gawd. That's what Calder meant. He could tell I was pregnant.

"Yes. It is too soon to know if it is a boy or girl, but either way, Tyrel will be staying nearby until you can take care of things on your own. Of course, you will never be alone. The entire Pride will be here to support you. Twins run in our family. We might get lucky!" Her face lit up at the possibility of two grandchildren. "I can't wait to see the look on Otto's face when the two of you walk into the gathering. Gideon may have signed a contract, but the Pride knows that you cannot fight a true mate bond. Otto will have to accept the fact that you are mated for life."

Tyrel signed and reached for Gwen's hand. There was one possibility no one wanted to bring up. "He might try to claim his contractual rights anyway."

"With her pregnant? Why would he bother? It will be at least a year and a half before she experiences heat again. How would he benefit?"

"He wants the Pride. He wants to be Gideon's heir. Forcing Gwen to honor her father's obligation may be his only opportunity to take control. Everyone knows Gideon is not going to remain in charge much longer."

Gwen wasn't sure what he meant but it didn't sound like something she wanted to hear. "Wait… wait just a minute. Forcing me to honor a contract I never signed. No way. That fat bastard will never get a chance to touch me again. I will kill him first."

Tyrel laughed. "If there are any challenges to be met, I will be the one meeting them. You are not yet under the Pride's jurisdiction. You have never undergone the ceremony of binding and have no way to prove you are entitled to protection. That is something we need to take care of before we make any other plans. I do not trust Otto or any of his inner circle."

Anola nodded. "I can ride over to Cherokee tomorrow and speak to Jimmy Sawnooks. Otto asked him to officiate his binding and Jimmy turned him down. I get the feeling he will enjoy officiating this binding ceremony."

Gwen looked puzzled for a moment and then she said, " Cherokee? Is he Native American?"

"Yes. He was also my late husband's best friend. Jimmy was certain that staking Otto over a fire ant bed after covering his body with honey would persuade him to admit he had Tyrel killed. I had to convince him spending the rest of his life in jail for killing Otto would not bring Tyrel back."

Tyrel didn't mention that he knew his mother was secretly dating Jimmy. This was the perfect opportunity for her to drop by his home without drawing attention to her presence in Cherokee.

Gwen was still puzzled. "Don't take this the wrong way. I realize you are the experts and all I have to go on is hearsay. I thought the Cherokee do not believe in skin-walkers. There's not a word for them in their language. I know that because a good friend of mine is Navaho. She is always talking about native mythology. Shape changers and skinwalkers are her favorite mythical creatures."

Anola smiled. "You're right. You will never get any of the Tsalagi to admit there is anything like a human that can change into an animal form. That agreement was made between the Tsalagi and our ancestor's hundreds of years ago. The Tsalagi have kept their promise."

"That's right. No one will learn of our people from any member of the tribe." Tyrel grinned. "That doesn't mean we don't exist, just that the First People will never admit it."

"Do we have to have an official ceremony? Can't we just live together and skip all the formalities? I'm not sure I want to sign anything after finding out what my father did." Gwen meant every word of it. She would never sign anything in the future without having an attorney look at it first.

Tyrel wrapped her in his arms. "Silly woman. Claiming you as my mate is more than a marriage contract. While your father's blood grants you the protection of the Pride, being my true mate is an even stronger bond. No one would dare to touch you. Our people mate for life. You will be the mother of my children. My life is yours. Your needs are mine to fulfill, and your dreams are my aspirations. You are the Omega to my Alpha and I will tear the throat out anyone foolish enough to try and stand between us."

Despite being shaken to the core by Tyrel's statement, Gwen remained quiet throughout dinner. Tyrel, Herman and Anola chattered away about unimportant news and gossip, catching up on everything that had happened since they were last together. After a couple of hours, she excused herself, claiming fatigue and headed toward Ty's bedroom.

She lay in the darkness, thinking about everything that had happened and what the future might hold. Insecurity had always been an issue, partly because of her who her mother was, and partly because she had always felt she was not good enough to earn her father's love. That anxiety and lack of confidence had followed her throughout childhood and into college. Once she started dating, she always attracted the type of man that expected a subservient woman. Usually, those relationships ended badly...for her. Until now.

Tyrel wanted her exactly as she was. Unconditionally. Flaws and all. None of the other men had considered her good enough. What had changed? Outwardly she was still the same person. Had learning she was different made it easier to accept her flaws?

She flopped back on the bed and used her head to adjust her pillow. This was not a time to be thinking about her ex's. Nor was it time for dredging up the memories of every failed relationship she'd suffered through. Tyrel was offering her a lifetime commitment. So what if she had only known him a short time. Her cougar soul had already acknowledged him as her mate. Now she had to speak up and let him know how she was feeling. She knew what her heart was telling her; it was only a small dark corner of her mind that still held onto that tiny smidgen of doubt. Even though it was considered fast by today's standards, she knew he was everything she had ever wanted in a man. He was her life mate.

She took a deep breath. "Okay, let's do it."

Chapter 17

The dogs barking as the blue pickup pulled into the yard was the only warning Gwen and Tyrel received that they had visitors. "I'll put on some coffee," Gwen offered. She yawned and reached for her housecoat as he slipped into his jeans.

"Stay in bed and sleep. It's probably someone looking for my mother."

She mumbled something as she rolled back into a ball and pulled the blanket back up. Ty could hear her soft snores begin as he walked toward the door, cursing whoever was there for waking him up. He was still recovering from the challenge injury and needed the late afternoon nap. He had no idea who was knocking at the door, but there were only a few people that dared to show up at this house unannounced.

Tyrel frowned. His mother had gone to Cherokee that morning to arrange for the ceremony and she had not yet returned home. Unfortunately, it was the one visitor that they could not ignore.

"Welcome back Tyrel," his smile was closer to a smirk than a grin. "Heard you found my daughter."

Tyrel rubbed his eyes. "More like she found me. But we ended up together."

"That's what I came to discuss. When did you get back?"

Ty looked at the clock on the wall above the fireplace. "About eight hours ago. Gwen is still sleeping. We were both exhausted and took a nap. Sit down and I will go get her. I will put on some coffee while she is getting dressed."

"Can it wait? I would like to talk to you first."

Ty nodded and they walked together into the kitchen. He flipped the button on the coffee maker, smiling when he saw his mother had left the machine setup.

"Coffee?"

"I could use a cup."

Ty filled two cups and set fresh cream and sugar on the table. There was a cinnamon nut ring coffee cake in a covered cake dome. He gestured toward the cake and Gideon cut himself a slice. "Anola always has made the best coffee cakes around."

Ty waited until Gideon had taken a sip and eaten a few bites of the cake before speaking. " So...what is it you want to talk about."

"You, Gwen. I am guessing by all the rumors I have been hearing, you and my daughter have bonded. I am also assuming that means I will be a grandfather soon. What are your intentions?"

"Haven't thought much about it. This was not in my immediate plans. But it does change a lot." He ran his fingers through his fingers and signed. "My mother is already plotting my downfall. She mentioned a spot by the lake that would be perfect for a house. "

"I assumed she would be. She's been wanting a grandbaby for years. She would build the house by herself if she thought it would entice you into moving next door. And she hates Otto. There is no way she will sit back and watch him destroy everything your father built."

"I haven't had a chance to discuss that with Gwen. She was really upset over the injuries I sustained during the heat challenges. Not sure how she is going to handle another challenge fight."

"Don't mention it. Stay away from town and heal as long as possible. Wait him out. There is no way Otto will let me retire without a challenge. By now, he's planning something to take you out of the equation. Make sure you check your truck carefully. You know what happened to your father."

"I won't make that mistake," Ty stated flatly.

"What mistake?" Kate stood in the doorway to the kitchen, a puzzled look on her face. "Why did you let me sleep so long?"

"Because you needed it. You didn't get much rest last night."

"I'm fine. Hello father. What brings you here?"

Gideon cringed at the cold tone of her voice. " Just wanted* to see my baby girl."

Baby girl. He hadn't called her that in a long time. Gwen was still a bit unsure what she'd walked into. She looked around the room. Tyrel was sitting comfortably at the kitchen table, his long legs sticking out in front of him. His father was equally as relaxed. "Am I interrupting?"

Ty gave her a toothy smile. "Never. We were just discussing some of the latest gossip."

"Hmmm. I hate to interrupt male bonding but I'm famished. I can't believe how hungry I am."

"That's normal when you are pregnant. Mom must have been baking all morning, there's fresh coffee cake on the table. Want a cup of coffee?"

She nodded and sat down at the table.

While Ty was getting her coffee her father turned to her. "Actually, I was wondering if I could have a word with you in private. I have a few things I need to tell you."

"There's nothing you can say to me that you can't say in front of Tyrel. It looks like you and Ty get along. There's no need for a private conversation."

Gideon looked uncomfortable but he didn't argue the point.

Gwen changed the subject and asked Tyrel, "How are you feeling? Do you feel like anything is not healing correctly? I can't forget how that little piece of metal kept your arm from healing. "

"The meds wore off, and the pain is starting to be annoying. I took one of the blue pills doc gave me, but it didn't help. I think something stronger may be needed."

"It has only been two days since you were hurt. Despite the accelerated rate of healing, I would be more surprised if you didn't need a pain med. Doc said you could have another one of the blue pills if you need it. The red ones are for late at night because they will make you sleepy. She also said you should shift at least twice a day."

"I know. I'm just being lazy."

Gwen furrowed her brow. "Maybe we can go hunting later. I am craving something and I can't figure out what it is. I can't get my mind off freshly killed meat."

"Talk to Anola. She might know what your body is craving. I want you to realize you are now part of a small, very tight-knit community. There is a level of comfort exercised with one another that cannot be explained outside of the concept of a Pride. All of the women will want to mother you. Besides being typical southern women, a lot of them are mothers and grandmothers who no longer have anybody at home to spoil. You are a prime candidate for their attention in their eyes. You need to be nursed through your pregnancy with good food and lots of mothering. It will be nothing like your life before."

That's what Gwen was afraid of… She realized the conversation had come full circle and she was back to Gideon's earlier statement. "What was it you wanted to talk about?"

"Otto. By now he has heard you are bonded with Tyrel. He's going to want compensation. Hopefully, he will just want money. However, he may try to hold you to the contract anyway."

"There's no way in hell I'm having anything to do with him. Even if I weren't pregnant, you could not force me to let that man touch me again."

"He wants my position," Gideon said. "He knows I was voted into Pride leadership after Tyrel's father was killed. He knows I will be retiring soon. There's no way anyone will vote for Otto. So his only option is to challenge for leadership. I'm too old to defeat him in a fight. That means I would have to abdicate. Then the challengers will face each other. Otto's mean and he fights dirty. A lot of people expected Calder to challenge Otto when the time came. Now he's not going to be able to fight."

"Isn't there anyone else that could challenge him?" Gwen asked.

"There's only one Alpha in the area." His eyes went to Tyrel.

Gwen felt her stomach hit the floor.

***

Otto sat at a booth near the back of the restaurant talking with two of his men. The early morning rush had wound down and most everyone had gone home to sleep off the effects of the aborted search. Only Otto and his two most trusted allies were inside the 24-hour chain restaurant.

"So what are you going to do about it? Talk about handing someone their balls. Have you seen Calder? I've seen meat at the butcher's that didn't look as ground up as he does."

Otto studied Billy a moment before commenting. "I'm not sure yet. There's not a lot I can do about breaking a mate bond. The till death do us part complicates things."

Billy didn't reply. He signaled for the waitress and stared at the menu.

"I've never seen you nervous about a fight," Pete said.

Billy's eyes never left the menu.

"Fuck you. I'm not nervous about a fight. I'm just not sure if that is the best answer." Otto leaned back and let the young waitress lay silverware on the table. As the waitress walked away he muttered, "I could tear that ass up."

Billy laughed "Careful, she doesn't strike me as the type to fuck and fade."

A blue pickup pulled in and the passenger door opened. A busty blond wearing a denim miniskirt, a skintight tank, and no shoes got out, amid a steady stream of cursing. She was still screaming at the driver when he pulled away.

The young woman waited until he was out of sight, then used her hands to adjust her hair into some semblance of order, before entering the restaurant. She stood by the door a moment, studying the occupants, and then walked over to the booth where the three men sat.

"Hi, Otto. Billy. Pete. Want some company?"

She indicated she wanted to join them, but Otto made no effort to move. Billy continued to study the menu.

"Aren't you gonna scoot over and let me sit down, I'm really hungry," she asked in a pouty voice.

Otto turned to look at her. "How'd you get here?"

"With Micah, he had to run to the ATM."

"Then go outside and wait for Micah to feed your whining ass."

The woman sighed and took a seat at the counter next to the booth. She sat there without ordering anything until the same blue pickup pulled up and the driver blew his horn.

"There you go," Otto called out, "Micah's back. You got your ride home. If you're lucky he might stop and grab you a burger."

The woman gave him a eat shit and die glare. "Hmph," she huffed. Then she slid off the stool to catch her ride before Micah grew annoyed and pulled off without her.

A motorcycle was pulling in as she was walking out. The driver parked, set his helmet on the bike's seat and walked toward the restaurant. He held the door for the woman to leave then went to the booth where the brothers sat, turned a chair around at the end of the booth, and straddled it.

"Hungry?" Otto asked.

"Yeah. My ass is still vibrating from the ride up," TJ replied. "Ol' lady forgot to leave me the bank card."

Otto took a long leather wallet from his back pocket and unhooked it from his belt. He tossed it to TJ.

"Take what you need."

TJ caught it and nodded, removing a twenty before tossing it back. He signaled to the waitress, ordered a T-bone, medium, and eggs, scrambled with cheese, with hash browns scattered and covered.

The waitress set down the cup she was carrying and filled it, before refilling the ones before the other two men. "You guys eating?"

"Yeah, make mine rare. Billy's medium rare, eggs over medium."

"What about you Pete?"

"Ol' lady's birthday. Gotta take her out for dinner. I'll take another slice of apple pie. Heat it on the grill and melt some cheese on it."

Otto waited until she'd walked off to call the order, then said, "Things are changing fast. Now that the bitch ran off with Tyrel, it's gonna block a lot of the expansion I had hoped for. That sucks too since Gringo wants to double our weekly distribution."

"And what 'cha gonna do about it?" TJ prompted.

"Who's the best I can call in to take care of the problem? Gringo promises to up our percentage to thirty and I ain't going to give up that much cash because of a woman."

Billy nodded his approval. "Truth. We were just discussing the available local options when you pulled up. Gideon can't stand for a challenge and keep everyone thinking he's unable to shift. It's going to take out of town talent. Can't risk anyone recognizing the scent. Tyrel is still in his month of recovery, so he is in no shape to fight. Calder is down for at least three months."

"So, if you take out Gideon there won't be anyone around to challenge?"

"No, that would only force another vote. I spent quite a bit of time last night thinking about the best way to handle it. I want someone good enough to put Gideon in a bed, but not kill him. That will open up the discussion about his age, his health, and his ability to lead. Once I get an opening, Billy or Paul can recommend he abdicate. That will force a challenge."

"What you going to do about the daughter?" TJ asked.

"She's already bedded and bearing. She's going to have to wait. A lot of things can happen in a year. Once I take over as Pride leader, I will ensure Tyrel will never be a problem again," Otto replied."

TJ leaned back, with his head against his crossed arms.

Billy broke out laughing. "Why wait for her to whelp? If you don't want to take care of it, I will do it."

"Let TJ take care of it. You don't need any more problems after the blowout last summer. TJ's a bit more diplomatic than either of us. If he thinks he can find someone from out of town to do it, that would be best. That way we can all be at the tavern with lots of witnesses. It's best we don't get involved."

He stopped talking as the waitress arrived with platters of food. She filled all the coffee cups, got TJ another coke, and asked if any of the men needed anything else. Billy opened his mouth to make a lewd suggestion but Otto kicked him under the table. He shut his mouth and picked up his fork.

The four men dug into their breakfast.

Chapter 18

Gwen lay in their room, looking at an owl that was hunting for dinner in the field outside the window. Though they had been there for several days, Tyrel had made no effort to make love to her. She found herself wondering if the only time her people enjoyed sex, was when the woman was in heat. That idea sucked. It was so fast, but she knew Tyrel was everything had ever wanted and the only man she would ever want again. Now that she had experienced how great sex could be, she had no intention of waiting until after this baby was born. Her mate was not making it any easier.

Hair still damp from his shower, Ty walked back into the bedroom, moving with the lethal grace of a predator, a grace that brought a tightening to her pelvis and hardened her nipples.

Tyrel was wearing a towel, thankfully. If not, Gwen knew she would probably have lost the ability to speak. It clung to him like a second skin, showcasing his muscular legs and washboard stomach, the wet cotton tight enough to show the curves of his cheeks as he walked across the room. He had taken the time to comb his long dark hair back away from his face but he had not braided it. Ty approached the bed slowly, his every step exact and full of purpose. She loved watching him; his lithe body moving and flexing with each step. He was the embodiment of his cougar… and he was her mate. She was surprised by how good that made her feel. It was a physical thing, a searing river of fire winding through her blood, setting every nerve ending alight. Tyrel exuded hot and sexy male, and her hormones were reacting exactly as she feared they would. No, you will not seduce him. No. No. Fuck it. Yes!

Just thinking about Ty made her nipples tight and hard. Whenever he was near her now, she had to clench her thighs to slow the moisture.

Tyrel laughed a soft chuckle that added to her shivers. "You do realize I can smell the changes in your body now. You can't hide your excitement and I love it." He could easily see the delicate pink of her pert nipples tighten against the creamy beige of her firm breasts. Once again, he groaned at the eager stirring of the erection he'd fought so hard to control. Fuck, Fuck, Fuuuck. Think of something else. Quick." Got anything to drink?" He was suffering from a bad case of dry mouth. A beer would be great. Crown would be better, but any bourbon would be fine. It would help to settle his nerves. Just thinking about Gwen had him trembling like a teenage boy on his first date.

"Not really." She needed something much stronger than a beer herself. The small amount of ice left from her glass of tea was not going to do the trick. "Didn't I see a bottle of something on the shelf in the closet?"

"Hang on and I will check." He walked to the closet and returned carrying a bottle with a few inches of golden caramel Tennessee whiskey inside. "Not a lot, but enough to have a drink. Want yours over your ice?"

She nodded and Ty poured a generous shot into her tea glass. Then he turned the bottle up and drank about half of the remainder.

"That's better," he said with a grin.

At least her mind was now on something other than jumping his bones. It would be a hell of a lot easier if Tyrel were wearing more than a towel around his waist. The way the towel draped low across his groin and hips had her attention She used her eyes to trace the tribal tattoos that decorated both of his arms, his muscular chest and shoulders, and parts of his back. There was even the top of one peeking over the towel he wore around his waist. They only added to his virality. She wanted to trace them with her tongue, then follow the washboard stomach down the six-pack to explore the tempting bulge she could easily see hiding behind the towel. It surprised her to feel these kinds of urges…but since she had bonded with Ty, she had been experiencing emotions and desires she had never experienced. He had said it was normal but Gwen had never heard any of her friends back home discussing anything like it. And her friends talked about everything… in detail.

He walked toward the bed and she closed her eyes, knowing that once she looked into his sultry gaze, all her defenses would fall. She could feel his presence beside her, near enough that she could hear him breathing, an intense awareness of a predatory male within her personal space, but she didn't want him to move away. When he put his hands on her shoulder, a shiver ran down her spine. Her heart began to beat faster as her body reacted to his touch. His lips sought hers, the kiss wet and demanding. Their tongues stroked and parried each other in an intimate ages old dance of 'give a little, take a little'. Her arms locked around his neck, pulling him closer, kissing him passionately. She clung to him like a drowning man clinging to a floating spar, knowing the water-soaked wood could sink at any moment, but realizing it was her only chance at survival.

Gwen had never dreamed a man's kiss could be so powerful, so erotic. His lips were firm, his tongue hard and demanding. When he reached for her, she rose to meet him, her body silently demanding his touch. He heard her moans as his hands caressed her body, lingering for just a second on each aching breast before moving down to take one firm cheek in each hand. She reacted by arching upward, eager to feel his lips and tongue again. He was happy to oblige her.

Within a few minutes, she became more aggressive in her demands. She threw her head back, extending her neck, practically purring in his arms as she leaned back against his muscular chest, rubbing against him like a cat in heat. She could feel the hard bulge of his erection pressed against her ass, and it was all she could do not to gyrate her hips against him. He had to know what she was feeling, the heady scent of her arousal wafted in the air. She wanted him to kiss and lick her all over, starting with her neck and her breast and working his way down her body until he reached the sweet spot between her thighs. At the slightest pulse of movement from his cock, she could feel her clit pulse and her muscles clench.

Once again, he ran the tip of his tongue lightly over her nipple, sending an immediate twinge of pleasure deep within her loins. Seeing her eyes closing and her expression soften as he mouthed her nipple, he began an earnest attack, flicking the tip, circling round and round, and then suckling, softly at first, and then with increased pressure. Her breathing was timed to her heartbeat, his breathing was becoming faster and harsher, slowing only as he suckled each nipple in turn.

Smiling wickedly, he circled her navel with his tongue. She reacted arching upward, eager to feel even more. Warmth flushed over her body as his hands moved to brush across her breasts before coming to rest against her rapidly tightening nipples. He began a slow circular massage, rolling her nipples between his thumb and forefinger. She closed her eyes enjoying the waves of pleasure coursing through her body.

Reacting to her response, he moved his hands gradually downward, acquainting himself with every nook and curve. Her body moved in a reflexive dance of anticipation. Seconds later his hand was moving again, down across her belly, around to cup each cheek again, kneading each one between his fingers. With each circle, his thumbs came closer and closer to the cleft between her legs. Her hips began arching upward, matching the rhythm in a desperate dance of desire. Finally, when she thought she would explode in anticipation his thumbs opened and explored her, probing and stroking until her body exploded in waves of pleasure.

Before the spasms ended he shifted downward, and she jerked away, crying "No", before her body betrayed her, clamping down against his shoulders as his kisses replaced his hands, driving away all her objections. When he finally flicked her button with his tongue, she trembled and begged for more. Confident of his talent, his tongue circled and probed relentlessly, until she was racked by waves of pleasure.

Before he could move away she reached for him, guiding his swollen cock between her thighs. With a muffled groan he entered her, hard and impossibly large, moving in long, slow strokes, to allow her body to adjust and her passion to grow. Then, with deliberate care, he increased the pace, varying his strokes, deeper for a few moments, then driving himself into her, then slowly teasing her until she begged for more. She bit down upon his shoulder, increasing her hip movements, matching thrust to thrust as he stroked faster, loving how she grew wetter with each plunge. His kisses rained down across her body, her neck, her shoulders, and finally her mouth, his tongue hard and deep, demanding she release herself to him once more. Shudders swept through her body. She dug her nails into his shoulder, pulling him ever closer, thrusting upward against his as her body contracted violently. The muscles in his forearms coiled so tightly, she wondered if they might snap. Twice more he pumped into her, hard and deep, then he gasped, and gradually slowed. They lay entangled, as their breathing returned to normal, and their bodies relaxed into sleep.

***

Gwen's eyes flew open. She didn't know what had awoken her. It wasn't a dream. She didn't smell smoke, and Tyrel had not touched her. Yet something had yanked her from a deep sleep. She frantically scanned the room. Nothing seemed out of place. She laid still as a statue, listening for any clue. Then she heard it: Someone was knocking on the door downstairs. It had to be someone the dog know because he had not barked.

Tyrel was already slipping his jeans on.

"Wait here, I will be right back." He padded downstairs in his bare feet, expecting to find his mother had locked herself out of the house. Or maybe it was his Uncle Herman.

He was back in minutes, a grim expression on his face.

"Get dressed. Hurry. It's your father. He's been shot."

Chapter 19

Gwen twisted her hands together and then wiped the excess antiseptic from her hands with the wipes the hospital provided.

Courtrooms and Hospitals made her nervous. She had no idea why; maybe it was the silence. It was oppressive. Anytime she was in one, she had to fight down the urge to say something, anything to fill in the emptiness. This one gave her the same feeling. She hated hospitals. It seemed like the only time he'd been inside one someone died. Or someone almost died but ended up changing after they got out, so it was as if they had died. At least there had been an empty parking spot near the door. Tyrel didn't like leaving his truck unattended. It would be too easy to rig some kind of 'accident'. They didn't know a lot of details about the shooting. After stabilizing his visible injuries, her father had been transported by ambulance to Merciful Sisters Hospital, where he was admitted for gunshot wounds and a temporal lesion with inclusions. Unfortunately, the shooting had happened in a Walmart parking lot, and there were too many people around for them to spirit him away to the Pride doctor. Mike was on staff and would be taking care of him but while he was in the ICU there were other people involved. Luckily, the chief medical technologist was one of the Pride and she was able to make sure his blood test results did not wave any red flags. The biggest fear was that he would wake up and not be aware. A mountain lion suddenly appearing in the ICU would be hard to explain.

Like most hospitals, this one was laid out in an exaggerated H design, with a thicker middle section and rooms ranged along both sides of the wings. The ICU was on the third floor and could only be reached by passing through an electronic door system. The attending physician, Doctor Miller, was making his rounds as he arrived, so they had no trouble getting updated information…not that it was of much help.

"Your father is stable but still unconscious from the surgery. When he fell, he struck his head against a rock. The swelling in the temporal lobe deadened the feeling on the left side of his body, which kept the pain from the gunshot from overcoming him and allowed him to walk into the building before he collapsed."

Gwen shivered. The agony he had endured to escape must have been severe. She had trouble imagining walking three feet with a bullet in his back, much less across a parking lot, but he somehow managed to make it. He had struck his head when he fell but at least he was where someone could call for an ambulance.

The doctors at Mercy put him in a medically induced coma to induce healing. That worked for now, but as long as he remained in intensive care, he was not safe. Critical care patients were observed too closely for anyone not to notice the accelerated healing factor. Mike would be transferring him to the private facility as soon as he was able to be moved. Because of HIPPA, hospital policy would not allow anyone except immediate family visitation rights, and then only after producing identification and proof of relationship. Once he regained consciousness things would change in a hurry, but for now, he was safe.

"Anything we should know?" Tyrel was hoping Mike would give him some specific answers. He was taking a big chance already coming to the hospital. The only way to ensure he was safe was to keep anyone from knowing where Gideon was. Plus there was a possibility that whoever shot him, also intended to shoot Gwen.

"Nothing. But that's to be expected. You do understand there is the possibility he will not wake up until we get him away from here? I have no way to give him a transfusion and the human blood is not helping him at all." He looked at me as I walked out of the room and then he smiled. My identity was evidently not a secret.

"Let us know if anything changes. Especially if he wakes up. He may have seen whoever shot him."

"Of course. I will leave orders to get word to you immediately. Of course, as the police are involved, we must notify them first. Other than the obvious, is there anything they should not know about the patient?" Mike made a brief examination and made a few notations on his chart.

"I would avoid anything that is not necessary. Make sure no one is to be allowed near him. I noticed they have a security officer near the entrance. I'm sure he is adequate to ensure he is not disturbed." Mike didn't need to worry about what was being said, but he still needed to be careful. HIPPA regulations would force the staff into silence/

The officer stationed at the door was a member of another Pride. So was the nurse assigned to Gideon. That's why they were happy he was at Mercy. The Federal Confidentiality Decree would prevent anyone from discussing an open investigation. But neither would stop the hysterics if Gideon shifted in the crowded room.

Satisfied there was nothing further he could do, and no one would be able to get near Gideon with the guard sitting right outside the entrance door, Ty nodded to the officer on duty and they left the hospital. Gideon was listed under an alias and his records were not included in the general public database. But it was a simple thing to verify, and simple was not good when dealing with an assassin.

***

"We have one more stop to make before we head home," Tyrel said as they were pulling out of the Hospital driveway.

"Really, why?" Gwen wanted to go home. The stress of the day was beginning to take its toll. She was exhausted and hungry. The baby had already accelerated her metabolism and she was eating more than normal.

"Mike told me there's a meeting being held to discuss your father's injury and the way forward for the Pride. I need to stop by and talk to a few people. Besides, it will allow you to meet some of your new extended family."

Wonderful…

The main room of the tavern was once again packed with people of all ages. Several lively conversations echoed around the room. Someone had dropped a few dollars in the jukebox, and Lynyrd Skynyrd was blaring in the background. The men gathered together into separate groups, laughing and joking together.

They all looked our way when we entered. No one appeared surprised to see Tyrel. One of the men looked her up and down, and then made some comment that made the others laugh. Even without hearing it, Gwen was certain it was about her…and it probably wasn't flattering.

All the women present were sitting together in one corner of the room, quietly talking amongst themselves. Two little boys sat at their feet, playing with miniature cars. None of the looks they gave her, made her feel welcome, but then again none seemed blatantly unwelcome. It was more of a wait and see attitude.

"Tyrel!" An excited voice came from the direction of the long mahogany bar, followed by an extremely pretty, petite young woman. She obviously didn't follow the no public display of affection rule. After enveloping him in a hug, she kissed him soundly on his cheek. Noticing Gwen for the first time, she raised an eyebrow in silent inquiry.

Tyrel laughed. "Gwen, this is Ella, my favorite cousin and the bartender of this fine establishment."

"Ella, this is my new mate Gwen. No other information will be forthcoming. So, don't bother asking."

Ella giggled. "Yeah, in your dreams." She nodded to an empty place in the row of stools along the bar. "Just flop down anywhere you can find a clear spot. We used to try and keep some type of order, but the men always end up in one corner and the women in the other. She winked. "It gives us a chance to decide on how they're going to vote without their interference."

Gwen laughed.

Just as Ella had warned, after their introduction, Tyrel muttered something about Mike and the twins and disappeared, leaving her alone with Ella.

Gwen was instantly overcome with a nervous fluttering sensation in the region of her stomach. The stool at the bar was no longer vacant. She looked around, seeing no place to sit except in the corner with the other women.

Ella came to her rescue.

"Come on, I'll introduce you around. I think everyone is in shock. No one thought Tyrel would ever find a mate, especially one that was not raised in a Pride. I think we were all prepared for someone entirely different. You are a pleasant surprise."

Her words made Gwen feel a little better but the major test was about to come. She wished Morgan or Anola would arrive. It would ease the pressure.

Ella led her over to the other women and introduced her around.

Gwen was pleased to see the cautious expressions had vanished. Except for one. A puzzled look came over her features and she looked her up and down, studying her, sizing her up. The look she gave her when she finished could have frozen fire. Somehow, she made an enemy, but she had no idea why. The woman was too old to be interested in Tyrel, so it couldn't be jealousy. She made a mental note to ask Tyrel about it later.

The women's conversation turned to normal things, the children, family life, their husbands, and jobs, the normal conversations women had whenever they got together. Of course, there were a few risqué jokes about Gwen's recent bonding, her mate, and the heated honeymoon that followed. She was the only recently bonded woman present.

The young single women did not have a say in Pride business and were not present. She would meet them all at the actual ceremony, which was to take place in three days. Ella was single but because of her job, she was allowed to attend the meetings. Gwen got the feeling Ella would have showed up anyway.

Michael, Ty's friend, was the handsome young doctor she had met at the Hospital. The two men had met when Tyrel had traveled to Oklahoma a few years earlier to take a class for one of his pilot certifications. His car had broken down in the middle of nowhere. Unused to the wide-open spaces of the desert and faced with steadily graying skies and the sound of distant thunder, Ty had started walking down the highway, determined not to be late for his class. When Michael spotted him plodding steadily along the empty road, he was soaking wet from sweat, exhausted and filthy. He had passed him a bottle of water, and they had driven the remaining three miles together. They became close friends.

After leaving the service, Mike had relocated to the area and now ran the Prides community clinic. He had met and fallen in love with one of Tyrel's cousins. Marriage outside the prides was not common, but it was not unheard of. Despite not being a shifter, Mike and Becca bonded and were the parents of the two adorable little boys, one that already showed signs of being a possible alpha.

Tyrel was standing next to Michael talking to twin brothers with muscular builds, both massive enough to be offensive linebackers on any major league team. For some reason, she had always thought of Native Americans as short and slender, but only one of the men present could be described in that way. Most of the men had been friends since birth. One of the twins must have said something about her, because Tyrel looked her way, threw his head back, and laughed out loud. She wondered what he found so funny.

The crowd was growing larger and she expected the meeting to start soon. Tyrel had been talking to most of the men and wondered what they were discussing. She saw him say something to two of the Pride elders and shake hands, then he walked over to the group of women and made his excuses, apologizing while explaining it was time for them to take off.

Gwen looked at him and frowned, wondering why he was ready to leave now when the meeting had not even started.

Tyrel winked at her but did not say anything.

One older woman he kissed on the cheek and whispered, "I listened to my cat."

"Finally." His grandmother scolded him for staying away so long and made him promise to bring Gwen back to visit her before allowing them to escape.

"Of course, Mee-maw. I promise to visit you soon."

"So many times, I've heard those words from you. I will see you when the wind blows you this way. In the meanwhile, go with my love and blessing." She turned to Gwen. Pulling her aside she whispered. "Tyrel's time to run with the rogues has drawn to an end. Now he must step up and take his rightful place. You must encourage him." She patted Gwen's tummy. "This kit will be a strong one. His father will have his hands full. He can handle it A reformed rogue always makes the best family man."

Gwen felt her face turning red. She was skeptical about the older woman's advice but considering her recent run of luck, she figured what the hell. At least the women of the family were on her side. Most considered Tyrel to be the perfect mate, tall, handsome, and an alpha male. His arrogance and intensity were considered assets.

As they were walking toward the door, she noticed the clock over the mantle said it was just before eleven o'clock, they had been there for over three hours.

Tyrel didn't speak until they reached the divided highway above the tavern.

"That truck we just passed was Otto. He is on his way to the meeting. It's scheduled to start at eleven. The elders decided it would be best if I was not present. This serves a double purpose. It leaves Otto wondering what I discussed with the elders. And it prevents him from issuing any type of challenge before I'm fully healed."

"Why would he want to challenge you?"

"He wants you to honor the contract."

"No way. We are mated. Doesn't he understand the 'til death do us part'?"

"He understands. That's why the challenge."

She thought for a moment. "Oh…."

***

Gideon opened his eyes and winced. He looked around the room, taking in the oxygen equipment, the IVs in his arm, and the television mounted overhead.

Not home.

Not the clinic.

Hospital.

How did he get to a hospital?

231

The blur in his vision was gradually fading as his eyes adjusted to the artificially bright light. It was a hospital room, no one in his family would ever paint a bedroom such a sickening pea green color. Nor would they allow a metal hospital bed with side rails in their home. He had no memory of how he got here. None. The last thing he remembered was parking the truck at Walmart and starting toward the door.

He wondered where all the nurses were. The only time he had been in the hospital, they were everywhere. Looking around, he noticed a call button on the head of his bed and pushed it, expecting someone to answer his page. After a minute he began to get aggravated. Why wasn't anyone answering him?

He was just about to try pushing the button again when a young woman dressed in a nurse's uniform showed up. She walked over and pushed a button on the machine with the annoying beep, and it finally stopped making that annoying noise. Without saying a word to Gideon, she glanced at her watch, made a notation on the clipboard lying on a table beside the bed, offered him a slight smile, and then left the room, placing the clipboard in a bin attached to the door on her way out.

It was evident she had no intention of answering any questions. He could hear her talking to someone just outside the room, but he could not make out what they were saying. In frustration, Gideon snatched the thin pillow from behind his head and tossed it out the door.

This time when the nurse entered the room, the expression on her face had changed from placid neutrality to one of shocked disapproval.

"You must be feeling better," she said as she raised my head and slipped the offending pillow back into its normal position.

"Where am I," he asked again, not that he was expecting an answer, but figured it was worth a shot.

Just for a moment, her eyes softened. "Dr. Miller is on the way." She left, closing the door behind her.

Still no answer to my question. He knew that nurses were trained not to answer questions. Some hippo rule, or something like that. He decided to give Mike Miller a few minutes to arrive before he unhooked the thingy from his arm and started looking for someone with enough authority to answer his questions. His head was beginning to feel like the bass drummer in the school band was warming up for a solo of Wipeout. He didn't know if he could handle the complete song.

Just as he was resigning himself to the possibility of really having to make a break for it, the door to his room opened and a familiar face walked in.

The smirk on the doctor's face irritated him. Mike would think it was hilarious seeing him lying in that bed.

"I'm glad to see you. What the hell am I doing in a hospital?" He was practically screaming; his body was shaking, and his hands were trembling. Somewhere in the back of his mind, his cat kept saying, it's alright. They are just trying to help you.

"Your stubborn ass got shot in the Walmart parking lot. I assume it wasn't a robbery."

"Damn. I must have been out of it. No way you can get me out of here?"

"I can now that you are awake. You've been lying unconscious in the ICU for three days."

"Three days? For a bullet?" Gideon couldn't remember much but the longer he was awake, the clearer things became. He was definitely in the Hospital. He could see high rise buildings out the window, so he had to be in a city. He had no memory of riding in an ambulance, but Mike had said something about them getting him here as fast as possible. But wasn't he healing? He had been shot before and the wound usually closed and healed in a day or two.

"No. For the brain injury, you sustained when you tried walking to your car, fell and hit your head on the cement curb."

"And no one recognized me. ICU, huh? Tell me it's Mercy."

"You got lucky on that. They could have taken you somewhere else. Somewhere without a family member on staff. How are you feeling?"

"Fine. I don't remember much…well, I don't remember anything after parking the truck. They must have given me something for the pain that my body couldn't breakdown. You might want to look into that and see what kind of medicine they gave me."

Doctor Miller appeared shocked by my statement. "Chart says the doctors didn't give you anything. No pain meds, just fluids to keep you hydrated."

"That sucks. How did you get here so fast? I only woke up a little while ago."

"I've been here the whole time, waiting to see if you would wake up. Well, I did take turns grabbing a few hours of sleep with Bridget but other than that, I've been right outside.

"That makes me feel better. I didn't do anything that might…"

"Can you be a bit more specific? Like, did you turn into a ravenous mountain lion and attack anyone?" He grinned and laid a finger aside his head as if he was thinking hard. "Nope."

"Smartass. I was really unconscious for three days?"

"Almost four. You might not remember much. The concussion was centered on the park of your brain that regulates sleep, so that's normal. You may also develop a type of PTSD."

Gideon didn't like the way that sounded. Anything that messed with his brain scared him. Shifters did not survive long with brain damage. It was too dangerous for the pride to allow them to live.

"Things are a bit blurry." There's no way I'm going to admit to anything else.

"I'm glad you are okay. It was touch and go for a while. I got you here as fast as I could but by the time I arrived the surgeon had already opened your skull to relieve the pressure...."

Mike didn't have to finish the sentence. Gideon realized he could have gone feral at any time. It was nothing less than a miracle nothing serious or life-changing had happened. He could imagine the news headlines if a mentally challenged cougar tore the operating room staff into bite-sized chunks. Not to mention the security guard's reaction when his dead body morphed back into human form after he the rampaging mountain lion.

"I had Rachel send word to Gwen that you were awake. I'm sure she will be here soon."

"Rachel. That my nurse? She's blood?"

Mike nodded.

"Good to know…Three days. That means they called in the council today."

"Yes. That's why Gwen and Ty are not here. Tyrel may not have wanted to be involved, but circumstances have changed. The attack on you could herald a similar attack on Gwen. He is not going to allow anyone to endanger his mate or his baby."

Mike moved away from the bed and stood by the window staring out at two pigeons walking along the window ledge. Gideon was curious about what the dour doctor was finding so fascinating, but a floor nurse came in and we both got quiet. As she took his vitals they chatted about random things.

"Glad to see you are still with us," Mike acted as if he had just arrived and this was the first time had a chance to talk to his patient.

"Takes more than a bullet to take me out, Doc. Hurts like the dickens though."

"I bet. Other than that, how are you feeling."

"Not bad. Ready to go home."

Mike laughed. " It's going to be a few more days. Rachel will be back in to change your bedding so I'm about to be run out of the room. Do you need anything?"

"Yes. My damn clothes."

"Not a chance ol' man. Just stay in bed and rest."

"Well at least get me a coke. Maybe two. And a Snickers bar. And try to call Ty and Gwen. Tell them to bring some Micky D's. A Big Mac and French fries sound so good. I'm starving."

Mike laughed and reached for the door. His eyes went to the young woman standing in the doorway. It wasn't Rachel. He cocked an eyebrow and she realized he had no idea who she was.

"Sorry doctor, I'm just here to give him an antibiotic," she replied.

Her words caught Gideon's attention. Since he wasn't sick, he had no idea why they were going to give him an antibiotic. He wanted answers … and the coke. What was Mike waiting on, a tip?

The nurse was rolling a small tray over to the bed. Then she filled a syringe with a thick white liquid. Gideon took one look at the syringe in the nurse's hand and that was it; his cougar started yowling. Something about the needle was rattling his subliminal memory.

Mike must have picked up on my emotions. "Wait!" He grabbed her arm just before she pushed the needle into the IV. "What' is that? It looks like penicillin."

"That's what was ordered. Penicillin."

It didn't mean a thing to Gideon, but Mike turned bright red and lunged at the startled nurse, grabbing her by the arm before she could push the plunger.

"No!" he was practically screaming. Gideon had never seen him react to anything like this. "Are you trying to kill him? He's allergic to Penicillin."

The young nurse looked puzzled, but she quickly checked the clipboard. "I'm sorry doctor. It doesn't say anything about Penicillin allergies."

Michael's face grew red. "I wrote the allergy information on his chart myself. Who ordered this antibiotic?'

Gideon was very interested in what the nurse had to say. Someone must have ordered the penicillin and changed his records. That did not make him want to remain in Mercy any longer than it took to order transport to the clinic.

"It says here Doctor M. Miller." She went pale and looked faint. Mike's name was clear to read on his lab coat, and she knew the short pudgy blonde haired man looked nothing like the tall, muscular black doctor standing before her. A doctor she had seen taking care of the patient for the last three days.

"Now that mention it, he was wearing a red band yesterday." The young nurse was puzzled. She was certain the patient had been wearing a medical alert bracelet when he was admitted to the floor. She needed to go and report this to her supervisor.

"Send Rachel in before you do," he replied as she walked away.

"Damn." Michael shut his mouth quickly and took a deep breath. Gideon could tell he had something he wanted to tell him but needed to wait until the nurse was well away before he did."

For some reason, Gideon wasn't upset. If what Michael said was true; it meant someone was still trying to kill him. He waited impatiently for the nurse to disappear down the hall. Then he pounced.

"Okay. Start from the beginning and give me all the gruesome details. But first, does the snack machine in the waiting room have cokes… and snickers?" He felt like an idiot asking that one.

Mike broke out laughing. "Yeah. I should have thought of that. You always have one with your coke."

"Yep. Get me one of those, too. Then get me transferred to the clinic. I'm not safe here."

"I'll be back as soon as I set up your transfer. Rachel should be right in." Mike left, mumbling something about training protocols and inexperienced nurses.

Gideon lay back on the bed and tried to relax. His Cougar was badgering his subconscious, You're in danger. Get out! Every nerve was on end. The slight creak of his door opening drew his attention. There was no way Mike had made it to the snack bar and back this quick.

His eyes went to the door. Standing just inside the room, was a short pudgy man in a doctor's white jacket, He was holding a black pistol with a silencer in his hand.

Without thinking, Gideon launched himself into a roll down the bed straight at the unwelcome visitor. They both went crashing to the floor, immediately followed by the stainless steel stand that was holding the bag still attached to his arm by the plastic IV lines. Gideon tried to grab the arm holding the gun, but for a small man, he was extremely strong, tossing him to the side without any visible sign of effort. His head hit something hard and everything blurred out. It must have opened up a cut because blood was trickling down his forehead into his left eye making it difficult to see. And he couldn't concentrate…again.

The noisy machine was beeping madly and someone had finally noticed something was wrong.

"Can I help yo…," As Rachel entered the room, Gideon grabbed her arm and missed. Then the fake doctor pointed his gun her way.

Rachel screamed and the clipboard she was carrying clattered to the floor.

No!!!! Gideon struggled to rise, but he was tangled in the IV line so that every time he moved the needle jabbed into his arm. Somehow he managed to throw himself in front of the young nurse, trying to shield her with his body. The bullet sliced across his right hip, splattering the nurse's crisp white uniform with warm blood. He knew it was only a matter of time before security arrived. Mike was running his way. He could hear his cougar yowling and it was pissed off.

The fake doctor wasn't hanging around to try again, he turned and ran past the screaming nurse out the room door.

Gideon reached for his IV, intending to pull the offending needle out of his arm. He must have blanked out for a second because when he looked again Michael was standing over him.

"Help me to my feet. There's no way I'm staying here I'm staying there after what had just happened. No matter what you say I am not getting back into that bed."

Mike didn't argue. " Here's your snickers. Eat it. Your coke is on the bed table. Give me time to get the ambulance here. He's not going to try again. Too many have seen his face. Security is searching the hospital for him now."

Gideon sat on the side of the bed watching the door after Mike left the room. Call it street smarts or gut instinct or old fashioned stubbornness, but he was leaving the hospital now regardless of what Mike said. First, he needed clothes, then shoes, and then he was out of here as soon as Gwen and Ty arrived. He could see the parking lot out the window and had seen Tyrel's truck pulling in.

What did they do with my clothes? Gideon searched the drawers of a side table, but it was empty.

So was the closet. Since he was wearing pajama's someone must have brought them…they would have to do. Pushing himself to his feet he took two steps forward then everything started spinning. He thought he heard Gwen call out his name, and he begged, "please get me out of here," then collapsed.

Chapter 20

Gwen pushed the wheelchair into the den, placing it so that Gideon could see out the window. "Michael going to drop by later to watch the game. Anola is making hot wings and a pizza. I need to put a load of laundry on. Will you be okay?"

"I'm fine. I will sit here and enjoy the view."

Gwen laughed. All he could see was the path down to the lake.

Once Michael had Gideon at the clinic he had completed an immediate blood transfusion. The potent red cells had stimulated his body to repair the damage the bullet had done. Unfortunately, the injury to his spine was more than one shift could repair. Damaged nerves healed slowly. It could be months before he was able to walk on his own.

After what happened at the clinic they were afraid Morgan was not enough to keep him safe. Tyrel had him brought home with them.

Earlier they had discussed what to do about Otto. Both men were certain the attack had not been random. The angle of the wound showed that the bullet had come from a ridge to the left of the parking lot. The only way to reach the ridge was to park by the hardware store and climb the rock face. Unfortunately, no one saw who had shot him and the hardware store did not have a camera set up to watch the parking lot.

"There's no way to prove it wasn't an accident. It could have been a hunter with lousy aim. It is deer season," Gwen said.

"Deer? No buck still able to walk on his own is coming anywhere close to this town and you know it. It had to be Otto."

Ty agreed but there was no way to tie him to the shooter. "He was sitting in the bar, drinking with Pate and Billy. There's no way he could have done it."

"There has to be a way to get out of the contract." Gwen refused to accept the possibility that she might be forced by Pride law to accept Otto as a mate. She still had not gone through the binding ceremony with Tyrel but that didn't matter. Ty would kill any man that touched her. The baby was moving now, and it was only a matter of months before she could him in her arms. Her morning sickness was over but would gladly suffer through it again if it kept Otto away. Just thinking of him disgusted her to the point that she was nauseous.

"Otto has challenged the validity of your bond with Tyrel and has petitioned the council to prevent the binding ceremony. Without it, you are not legally mated and you cannot be guaranteed the protection of the Pride. Your child may not be accepted into the family." Gideon was extremely upset that Otto had challenged their bond while she was pregnant with Ty's child.

"I don't understand how he can do this. Isn't there anything you can do? You are the Alpha."

"When an Alpha is unable to face a challenger, he has to abdicate. A challenge fight is a fight to the death. The bullet is too close to my spine to safely remove. In time, I might be able to shift safely, but it's also possible I may never be able to shift again."

"So you have to abdicate?"

"An old man in a wheelchair fighting a mountain lion to the death is not an attractive picture. The council is stalling but everyone knows it's just a matter of time before they have to appoint a new Pride Alpha."

"And Otto thinks he is the best choice to take your place?"

"Otto wants to be the Pride Alpha. Binding with you would give his claim to membership legitimacy. He has been allowed to live on Wolf Mountain and be a part of the community because he is of the blood. Your child is the key to achieving his desires. He is willing to wait until you go back into heat after the baby is born. But there is no way he will allow you to formalize the bond with Tyrel."

"Well, I don't care what he says about that piece of paper being a legal contract. I never signed it... I am already bonded with Ty. The Pride may not acknowledge it, but that does not change the fact. And what happened to 'til death do us part'?"

Tyrel had not said much during their conversation but he was listening and considering Gideons words. No one knew a lot about Otto. The older Alpha had appeared about five years earlier with Billy, who claimed he was a cousin. His blood tests had confirmed his DNA even though he had not been able to shift form. "My father didn't trust him. He was certain Otto was hiding something.

"Hiding something? I let alcohol blind me. Witnesses or not, there's no way Otto wasn't involved with you fathers accident," Gideon said. "The fat bastard was smirking as the police questioned the witnesses. He had an airtight alibi; he was at the tavern when it happened."

"He had the same alibi when you were shot. That's coincidence enough to make me suspicious."

Gwen nodded her head at Tyrel's words. "Why would a random man walk up and shoot you? Someone had to put them up to it."

Tyrel's gut instinct was that Otto had killed his father. Everyone knew how his father felt about the obnoxious outsider. He remembered the day his father died as if it were yesterday.

Anola had cooked a big dinner and his cousin Amelia had joined them. She had brought an envelope addressed to his father that had been delivered to her house by mistake. At dinner that day his father had claimed a detective he knew had discovered something troubling about Otto. He didn't go into details, but he intended to present the information to the Pride council the next day.

He had been killed on the way to the meeting. There was a storm that day, a windy thunderstorm that started around noon and continued throughout the afternoon. It was still raining sporadically as the sun set that evening. While traversing a particularly dangerous section of the mountain highway, his pickup had blown a tire, skidding off the pavement and over the drop off. The truck had continued to roll and bounce several times before coming to a stop at the bottom of the ravine. Then it had burst into fire, with Ty's father trapped inside. At first the investigators had ruled it an accident. This was later changed to a murder.

Tyrel had spoken to the police after they pulled the body from the truck. The tire that had blown was not melted by the fire. There was an obvious hole in the side of the tire. The bullet was still inside the tire. There was no match in the data base. After a short investigation, it was turned over to the cold case division and filed with the other unsolved cases.

Gwen could not blame Tyrel or Gideon for being suspicious of Otto's motives. Just being in the same room with the man set off her alarms. Somehow she had to find a way to break the contract. Hiring an attorney was out of the question, it wasn't the type of claim you settled in court. She had an uneasy feeling that she would regret any action she took, although at this moment she could not explain why.

When Calder pulled into the yard she gave up any attempt to hold a conversation until after the game. Mike was right behind him. She popped some popcorn and set it on the coffee table. Hands reached for the bowl but no one looked up.

Tyrel had healed from any injuries he had sustained during their unusual honeymoon. Calder had also recovered completely. The two men had become friends, spending a lot of time together since the fight. Over the last few days they had disappeared for hours at a time but she had no idea what they were up to.

She figured they were hunting. Ty had provided a steady supply of fresh meat, mostly small game but occasionally deer or beef. Yesterday Tyrel had brought home a freshly killed goat. Anola had not questioned where it had come from. It was easier not to ask.

She sat a platter of buffalo wings on the table along with four fresh beers. The four men were glued to their chairs, their eyes locked on the television screen. Until one of the teams scored they would remain oblivious.

"You see my purse?" she asked Ty during the next celebration. She had her cell phone but her purse wasn't on the counter where she usually left it. Anola might have moved it. She was gone to visit a friend, claiming she could stand being inside another Sunday afternoon.

"No. Perhaps you left it in the truck," Ty said without taking his eyes off the television screen.

"Dang, I bet I did. My arms were full of grocery bags. I'll go look." She rose from the sofa and walked out the door. No one noticed. The game was in overtime, and until it was over, they were worthless. Of course, Ty had parked as far away from the house as possible. He claimed it was good for her to walk as much as possible. He could take his opinions and shove them up where the sun doesn't shine. At least it wasn't raining.

She glanced in the window of the truck, spotting her purse on the floorboard by the gas pedal. With her belly, it would be easier to reach it from the other side of the truck. She walked around and opened the door, reaching inside. As she stood back up, a hand reached around her waist and pulled her against him. A different man used one hand to cover her mouth. Before she could react, she was jerked backwards into the tree line. A third man grabbed her feet, lifting her off the ground.

Somehow she needed to gain control and shift. She had never attempted it while being held, but she doubted any of the men were strong enough to hold an angry mountain lion. The men holding her were unfamiliar and human, but there was a familiar scent on their clothing. She could not remember where she had smelled it before, but she was certain it would come to her. In frustration, she kicked and bit at the hand across her mouth, drawing blood.

Gwen got out a brief screech as he jerked his arm away, but a different man shoved a round leather ball into her mouth, buckling the straps behind her head. She couldn't talk or scream and the rubber ball made it hard to breathe. In seconds she was secured. They used zip ties on her ankles and wrists, pulling them tight enough to cut the circulation. The pain made it difficult to concentrate. She continued to struggle as they threw her body into the back of a pickup and took off.

She had been kidnapped. And until the food ran out or the game was over, she doubted anyone would notice she was missing. Tears ran down her face but she could not make a sound. She screamed for Tyrel but he didn't answer her silent calls. Why had they taken her? The only person who would have a reason to abduct her was Otto. Did they work for him? She had no answers.

It was only a few moments before the truck pulled off the main highway onto a dirt or gravel road. They drove a short way and stopped. The motor was left running but the men got out of the cab. They dragged her from the truck bed by her feet, not caring that she struck her head on the tailgate before she hit the ground. No one spoke as they pulled across a small open meadow to a large pine tree. One man held her upright as a second man used rope to hold her body there. They had not removed her bindings or her clothes. She had no idea why they had tied her to a tree.

Until the first one punched her in the stomach.

She doubled up as severe pain radiated across her swollen stomach. One man held her against the tree, as the other two took turns punching her.

Why? Why were they doing this? Then it clicked. Her baby. They were trying to kill her baby. Anger made her begin to shift.

The bigger man laughed at her struggle. The he hit her with a wrench he had brought from the truck, disrupting her concentration. The pain from the wrench faded as the men's blows continued. After a particularly strong hit landed she felt like her stomach was tearing. Her cougar yowled as the life inside her faded away. Tears ran down her face.

The waves of severe pain continued until she began fading in and out of consciousness.

The blows to her groin and stomach continued long after she passed out.

Chapter 21

The shiny grey Tahoe slid to a stop.

Is that a woman?

The driver jumped out and ran to the tree where the body hang. The teenage boy was scared. What if whoever had done this was still hanging around, watching to see if anyone was crazy enough to try and help her? He touched her body, noticing she was still warm. She was still alive!

Instead of trying to help her, he jumped back into the Tahoe, put in in gear and peeled out. Once he reached the state highway at end of the dirt road he stopped and pulled out his cell phone. He hesitated. Did he want to call from his phone? No. There was a service station about half a mile down with a payphone. He headed that way.

***

Tyrel answered his cell phone on the second ring. "Talk to me."

It was Rick, one of the local police. "We found her. She's alive but it's not pretty."

"Where?"

"Kid called from The Minute Man Market. Said she was tied to a tree on the road to the quarry. We just pulled up. I've got an ambulance on the way."

"Be there in five minutes."

***

Tyrel pulled his truck onto the side of the road to allow the ambulance to pass, then made his way over to the small group standing next to the pine tree. He could smell the blood and urine long before he reached the tree. His stomach roiled, the muscles clinching into knots. His body was shaking as he walked over and looked at the crime scene. The CSI team had begun taking photos of the tree and the nearby ground . They asked him to step back away so he did not disturb the area. One was making molds of footprints.

Rick laid a hand on his shoulder. " Let's walk back toward your truck. She's lost blood but she's alright. They are taking her to the clinic. Mike is already there waiting for her arrive."

"How could someone do this? Why? Gwen never hurt anyone." Tyrel was searching for the scent of another shifter but other than Gwen the only scents were human.

"I have no idea why a group of men would kidnap and torture her. They beat her, first with their fists and then with a bat or a stick of some kind. She had small cuts and bruises but no outward injuries. The blood came from inside. She must have sustained several internal injuries."

"Internal? The baby!" Tyrel slumped against Rick , who put an arm around his shoulder as tears ran down his face.

Ricks eyes darkened and his face grew stark and cold. He had not considered that. But the blood could have been from a miscarriage. Mike would know once he completed the examination, but his gut instinct told him Tyrel was right. Now that he thought about it, there was one person who would be very happy if she had lost the baby. Otto could not claim contract rights until Gwen went back into heat. Instead of it taking at least a year, he was now looking at six to eight weeks. At this moment Tyrel was too upset to think about it, but that would not last. Once he ensured Gwen was safe, and that she would be alright, he would remember Otto.

"Why don't you head over to the clinic and talk to Mike. Lisa is on duty. She would have called me if there was any reason to contact you. I'm sure Gwen would like to see you. There's nothing you can do here. We can tell from the tracks there were three men in a pickup truck. But that's not enough to begin a search.

Tyrel nodded and grasped Ricks hand. If Mike gave Gwen a transfusion to stabilize her, she could be well enough to shift by now.

"Go ...there's nothing here to point to anyone in particular. I'm willing to bet a month's salary none of them were local. We will make molds of the tire tracks but I doubt it will give us much info. It's not a matched set so I doubt any of them came with the vehicle."

Tyrel cranked his truck. Minutes later he was pulling up at the clinic. Mike was waiting for him near the door.

"She's sleeping. I gave her a pretty big dose of morphine. It won't last long with her metabolism but it should let her get some rest while we wait for the test results," Mike said. "She moves everything with no problem, so I don't think there was any spinal injury. Maybe a cracked rib or two but they are healing. She might be laid up for a few days and sore as fuck, but she will get rid of most of that when she shifts." He paused and Tyrel braced himself for what he knew was coming. "She lost the baby."

"I expected that after what Rick told me. The important thing is she's going to be okay."

"Does Rick have any idea about what happened?"

"You know as much as I do. You were there. All four of us were immersed in the last minutes of the game. Until the buzzer sounded and we came back to reality, we didn't realize she had never come back inside. We had no idea anything was wrong."

Mike stood at the door as Tyrel did his own check of his mate, ensuring himself that she was resting easily and healing as they spoke. It wasn't that Ty doubted Mike, he simply needed to see for himself. He was still kicking himself for not realizing Gwen had been in danger. Once they discovered she was missing, both men had shifted and searched the area. Mike had found where the vehicle had been parked but there was no way to tell which way they had turned at the end of the road. He had alerted the Pride and the Tribal Police but no one had seen anything out of the ordinary. The idea that they had simply driven a few miles up the road to the old quarry road before they stopped and tortured her had never been considered. Now he was mentally torturing himself.

Mile waited until Tyrel had kissed Gwen on the forehead and they had left the room before speaking again. "Outside of the evident person, with the most obvious reasons, do you have any idea who might have a reason to hurt her?"

"Melena?" Tyrel asked.

"I was thinking of Otto, but Melena fits. The more I think about it, the more it points to him. We don't know anything about him. He could have a large group of friends outside the Pride from his previous life. He told us he had been asked to leave because the Pride's alpha felt he was infatuated with his mate. Maybe it was more than that."

Tyrel thought about what Mike had said. It was possible. Otto could have arranged for outside associates to come in and ensure Gwen lost the baby in a manner that no one could connect to him. This wasn't out of the question when it set plans into motion regarding the leadership of the Pride. No one had expected to deal with this until after the baby was born. It had certainly not been anything he considered. Now that she had lost the baby Otto would be able to force the council to act on the contract. "That's such a stretch. No one could be that sick...not even Otto."

"Power corrupts. And he wants power over the Pride. There's no way to know how far he would go to get it."

Tyrel didn't answer. Mike was naturally suspicious. He had not liked Otto from the moment he had been introduced. Tyrel had not paid much attention to him, other than noting how disrespectful he had been to his mother...until his father was killed. "I agree. Otto's number one on my list. It's too convenient that he is always surrounded by witnesses whenever anything happens. No one could be that lucky. Melena can be a bitch but she would never hurt anyone. Physically anyway. I could see her laying a few mental guilt trips on me, but there has never been any type of formal relationship between us. "

"Did you father ever look into it? I remember hearing someone say he was on the way to the council meeting when he was killed. He had called the meeting. Could it have had something to do with Otto?"

Ty shrugged. "If he did, he never mentioned it to me. Not that I was around much. My mind was on finishing my tour in the Army, getting my civilian pilots license and staying as far away from this part of my life as possible. Gwen threw a monkey wrench into the works."

"You should talk to Rick. See if he can find out anything about Otto. There may not be any way to link him to what happened to Gwen, but he might find out what your father knew that got him killed."

"That's sounds like a plan. I think I need to drop by and talk to Melena, too. Just to clear up any misconceptions. I should have don't it weeks ago."

"Should I reserve a bed for you?"

"That's a damn good question. I've seen her shoot. She doesn't miss."

"Maybe you should call her instead."

"She deserves more than that. But first, I'm going to go and keep my eye on Gwen. Hopefully, when she wakes up, she might remember something that will help us find the men who did this to her. And once we do, I'm going to show them why cats love to play with their prey before they kill it."

Chapter 22

Gideons black Ford F150 pulling into the yard surprised Tyrel. It was Wednesday, and he wasn't expected until Sunday. He dropped the axe next to the stack of firewood then waited on the porch as Gideon slid from behind the steering wheel and crossed the yard, walking without assistance for the first time.

The last few months had aged him. Once muscular shoulders now drooped like those of an old woman bearing a great burden. Instead of a vigorous man of fifty-five, Gideon looked closer to seventy, with a face that showed many years of accumulated pains and sorrows. He was able to stand and get out of the wheelchair, but walked with tired feet and a halting step, his hands outstretched as if he expected to fall at any time.

Tyrel waited as he fought to climb the stairs to the porch, knowing any attempt he made to help him would be seen as a reflection of his diminished capacity since he was shot.

"Great to see you up and around," Tyrel said. "Come on inside. Gwen's watching some kind of soap opera but it's about over."

Gideon smiled. Like her mother, his daughter loved the hour long serial shows, using them as a means to escape the everyday reality of life in the mountains. Since losing the baby, she had become more reclusive, preferring to remain inside the house instead of running and hunting in the forest with Tyrel. There was still a faint defiant glint in the green eyes that observed him as he shuffled across the room, so he continued to hope she would make a full recovery. She had been home from the clinic for over a week. Physically, she was completely healed. Unfortunately, the emotional damage remained. They had to trust that in time she would return to the carefree young woman who had appeared at his door five months ago.

He dreaded the information he was delivering, wishing there were any way he could avoid it. Unfortunately, it was something they had to know. He leaned backward in the oversize recliner, sighing as the pressure was removed from his lower back. Mike had not removed the bullet, claiming it was still pressing on his spine. He was able to shift and that helped move it away. But it was going to be a few more weeks before enough tissue had formed between the bullet and his spinal cord to make removing it safe.

Ty leaned forward. "Out with it. I know the only thing that would bring you out this late in the afternoon is bad news."

Gideons face fell. "Otto has made his move. Billy and Pete claimed a lack of confidence in my ability to maintain control of the Pride. They cited my refusal to enforce the contract now that you are no longer pregnant. Otto asked the council to uphold the terms as stated in the contract. His petition is that Gwen is not an official member of the Pride, and as an outsider, she does not have rights of refusal.

"That's too bad for him. I would cut his manhood off with a rusty knife before I let him touch me."

Tyrel and Gideon both flinched at the vehemence in Gwen's voice. Gideon figured he better finish the conversation fast. "Otto also states that Tyrel's right to claim you as a mate has not been certified by the council, and by Pride law your bonding is not legal. You have never gone through the Binding Ceremony."

Gwen stood up ."There's a simple cure for that. I will leave. Tyrel works out of town most of the time anyway. I can move to Atlanta and we can continue our life without the Pride." Her eyes went to Ty, then widened in surprise as he sadly shook his head.

"It's not that simple. You can't just walk away. You know too much about the community now. Most of the time the only way to leave the Pride is to die. Since we are bonded they know I would not allow you to be hurt. The only solution would be for both of us to be eliminated."

"Fuck this. There's no way in Hell I'm going to allow that fat bastard to touch me," she retorted. Her hands were trembling as she rose to her feet. "I would rather be dead." The two men were silent as she stomped into the bedroom, slamming the door behind her.

Anola came out of the kitchen to see what all the ruckus was about. She nodded to Gideon as she wiped her hands with the dishtowel she was holding. "What's wrong with Gwen?"

"Otto. He's filed a petition for rights."

"Someone needs to rip that man's throat out," she snarled. For a second her eyes darkened, then returned to their normal light brown color.

Tyrel stood. "Excuse me a moment. I need to check on Gwen."

Gideon nodded but Anola didn't say anything. She waited until Ty left the room and then asked, "When is the council meeting?"

"Tomorrow afternoon."

"They are not giving us much time to prepare. What will you say?"

"Look at me Anola. They are right. I'm not fit to lead the Pride. It may be years before I regain full use of my body, If ever. I could not survive a challenge fight at this time and everyone knows it."

Her eyes went to the bedroom door. "He never wanted his father's position."

"Things change. Maybe he feels different about things now that he's mated to Gwen. The Pride would follow him."

"What if he refuses?"

"I don't know. At one time we expected Calder to take my place. He says he is happy being his father's heir. The council may open it to all comers. I'm sure there has to be a few alpha's out there willing to relocate to North Carolina. I'm not sure if they have time to arrive."

"Strangers. That's all we need," she spat.

"All we can do is wait and see what happens tomorrow at the Council meeting. I will leave you to talk to him. Give me a call once he decides one way or another.

***

Gwen lay on the bed staring at the ceiling. It wasn't fair. In a matter of minutes her entire world had been turned upside down. After not hearing from him for over a month, she had assumed Otto had accepted her mate bond with Tyrel and moved on with his life. The idea that he was still trying to enforce it against her will left her numb. There had to be a way out. Tyrel had received the insurance money for his helicopter. His new one was ordered and would be ready in a couple of weeks.

The insurance company had also paid her claim for injuries she had sustained in the accident. She now had more than enough money to pay Otto for her father's loses during the card game. It was only money. Her mother had set up a trust fund for her that she would get when she turned twenty-five. The rest of her money was in the hands of an attorney who paid all her expenses at the nursing home. One day soon she hoped to move her closer to Wolf Mountain. Now she wasn't so sure that would ever happen.

Tyrel waited until she stopped slamming doors and stomping around the room before entering the room.

Gwen was pulling clothing out of her drawers and shoving it into her pack. When she realized there was no way she could get everything in the one bag, she got frustrated and threw it all on the floor.

"Do you have a pistol?"

Ty raised one eyebrow.

"A pistol I need a gun. Now."

"Why do you need a gun? You can turn into a mountain lion."

"I'm going to shoot him. I would rather go to jail than go to him."

"That's silly."

"So now I'm silly? I'm also crazy. And if the council tries to force me to mate with Otto, they will see how crazy I am. If I can't be with you, I will blow him away, and then kill myself. At least I will be with my baby." Tears ran down her face.

Gideon sat on the bed and gathered her into his arms without saying anything. He held her against his chest while she sobbed. He understood what she was feeling. He had been shocked by the love that had developed between them in such a short amount of time. There was zero chance he would allow the Pride to separate them. The timing sucked. He had expected they would have more time to get ready. Finding out that the council had called for a hearing in less than twenty four hours will force him to confront an aspect of his life he had avoided since his father died. He had faced this kind of emotional pain twice in his life, once when he had seen the burnt out remains of his father's truck, and then when he saw Gwen lying in the clinic bed. He never expected it would come down to a choice like this.

Tyrel only stopped rocking Gwen when the phone rang. He glanced at the screen, noticing it was Rick calling. Perhaps the police had found out something about Gwen's attackers. Hoping to get some good news for a change, Ty hit the green button. " Hello…"

Chapter 23

Gwen was overcome by a sense of DeJa'Vu as they topped the hill before the Tavern. Just as it was during the last council meeting, the parking lot was packed full of vehicles. The major difference was that the bar was empty. Instead, there was a steady flow of people walking down a path leading into the nearby forest.

Tyrel waited until Gwen had exchanged her heels for a pair of sturdy boots, then they joined the stream of community members heading toward the meeting location. Once they arrived they gathered together--- some in pairs, occasionally standing silently alone, but mostly in small groups. There was an undercurrent of electricity in the air, a feeling that something important was going to happen. Gwen could hear several conversations and gathered from the occasional bits and pieces of information that no one was certain why they had all been asked to attend. Others knew about Otto, Billy and Pete. Most didn't care, but one or two was worried about who the next Alpha would be. These were the same people who smiled warmly when Tyrel walked into the clearing.

Unlike most council meetings, there were three non-members present. Two they did not recognize, but by the badge on their shirts and the holstered guns he was confident they were some type of police officers. Rick was the third.

This surprised Tyrel as he hadn't talked to Rick since Gwen was kidnapped. He'd tried, leaving voice messages on his cell, but no callback. Rick was married to a member of the Pride; he was familiar with their secret. The two strangers were not under guard, nor was anyone acting as if they did not have a right to attend the meeting.

Tyrel could tell Gwen was curious about the strangers. "The country officer on the platform is Rick. No idea who the other two men officers are, but they have to be connected to the blood somehow. Either shifters themselves or married to one."

"Is it normal to have out of town cops at these meetings," she asked.

"Never saw one before. This could be the first time. It seems like are waiting for someone in particular to arrive before beginning. I saw Gideon so it's not him. Calder's here, too" Ty had his ideas about who they were waiting on. His eyes scanned the clearing and only a few people were missing... Otto and his sycophants.

He noticed that Calder's father was talking to Gideon. So were two of the unmated alphas from Three Claw Pride, over near Mars Hill. Word of Gideon's injury and a possible leadership challenge had spread. He wasn't certain that had anything to do with today's meeting. Gideon would have told him if that was on the docket. It could still be brought up, but it was doubtful anything would happen today. The most logical scenario was that they were here to get a good look at the possible competition. A soft murmur of voices traveled across the clearing as Otto and his trio of followers entered the clearing. Gideon walked to the front of the flat rock and motioned for silence.

"Looks like something will happen now," Gwen whispered.

Gideon had been talking to Rick and the other two men when Otto arrived. He nodded and approached the front of the flat rock Gideon had been standing on. Everyone turned to hear what he had to say.

"You were called here today for two reasons. First, Otto has filed a petition to have Tyrel and Gwen's bond set aside due to a previous contract. This is something we have never needed to address as it has never come up before. The contract is valid. I wrote it and signed it. Gwen, my daughter was fourteen and had no idea what I had done. Nor had she any idea she was of our blood. She found out what she was about to experience the day before her eighteenth birthday. I believe that surprise and fear of the unknown is why she ran away when she shifted. I sent Tyrel to find her, not knowing they would end up as mates. The bond was formed and Gwen conceived." He paused, letting the words sink. He didn't need to go into details. They understood the implications. Finally, he began speaking again. "What many of you do not know is that Otto refused to accept the bond. He wanted contract rights during Gwen's next heat. No one was in a rush since it was going to be at least eight months before the kit arrived. The day after he filed a petition for the bond to be set aside, someone, three strangers kidnapped Gwen from her front yard. They took her to the old quarry road, tied her to a tree and beat her until she lost the baby. This was ten days ago."

Voices rose in anger. Many called out questions without waiting to see if Gideon intended to answer any of them. Finally he managed to quiet them down.

"The council's decision is to honor any legal contract between members of our Pride. It is the nature of the Cougar to follow the laws of the Pride."

Otto and his men all began shouting and slapping each other in the back.

Gwen's face flamed, and she swore under her breath.

Tyrel had to hold her to keep her from walking away. He was certain something else was coming. He clamped his hand around her wrist and held on as Gideon approached the microphone once more.

"The only question the council could not answer is what to do when the claimant is not an official Pride member but lives among us. A decision was made to accept Otto into the Pride, as long as there was nothing in his previous Pride to prevent him from joining. Rick was asked to do a background check. He will speak today about what he discovered."

Gideon waiting for all the talking to die down. He had been watching Otto and the big man was no longer celebrating the council's decision. His eyes were locked on Rick and the two strangers.

"The second thing we need to address is about Gwen's kidnapping. Most of you already know Rick. I'd like to introduce you to Carl Duncan and Brett Davidson. They are with the Denver police. They are also members of the Blue Mountain Pride in Colorado." He stepped back and allowed the older detective to move to the microphone.

"I am detective Carl Duncan, Denver homicide. Officer Hicks submitted DNA samples for two unknown men to the national database. Both came back positive. One of the men, Tim White, is currently an occupant of the Cedar Hill Cemetery in Denver. He was shot and killed during a bar fight last week.

George Rogers aka Rocket was arrested along with two other men that we now have identified as members of the Crazy Eights Motorcycle Club. While they are not of the blood, they both have connections via marriage to the pride. Rogers had two outstanding warrants at the time of Whites death. One of the club members has made a deal to avoid jail time by providing evidence of a crime. This crime occurred here in North Carolina."

Every face was looking at the rock. You could have heard a pin drop.

The officer continued, "In exchange for a lesser sentence, the club member identified Tim White as the gunman who shot Gideon. He also claimed that the four men were hired to kidnap and torture a young woman until she miscarried. That woman was Gwen."

Everyone began talking at once. Tyrel's eyes went to Otto and his crew. The four men were huddled together. Otto was talking animatedly, using his hands to articulate the importance of the discussion. They were still talking when the second officer moved to the microphone.

"Hello. My name is Detective Brett Davidson. I am with the Denver police department, assigned to investigate a rape murder case that happened three years ago. This case was considered a cold case. Until three days ago we had no idea where to begin to look for our culprit. You can imagine our surprise when we found a hair belonging to our suspected killer on the jacket of the deceased Tim 'Rocket' White. A second hair was found on the passenger seat of Rocket's Forerunner. This hair matched the one we had collected from the deceased woman's body. An unusual hair of a color we had not seen before… except among those of the blood."

He stopped and took a drink from a bottle of water he had been holding. "DNA was matched against every current member of the Pride in Colorado, without success. There was nothing in the national database. The only lead we had was that the three men had been seen together in North Carolina two weeks ago. Now we have men crossing the state, testing all members.

"You are here now. Can't we give you the samples," one young man asked. It was clear the vast majority of the Pride were ready to donate right away.

"Unfortunately, we are not set up to take samples. Its slightly more complicated than a mouth swab. The subject would need to shift into his cat and let the officer remove a hair and place it into a sterile container."

Tyrel heard what he said but had other things on his mind. There was an enticing aroma floating in the air, a strangely familiar scent. That's when it hit him. It was Gwen. She was going into heat. Shit!

He breathed her sweet perfume deep into his lungs, visibly shaking as he struggled to force some type of coherent sound through clinched lips. Before he could stop it, a deep, guttural growl escaped. Every inch of his body tingled, the innate electric surge sending a rush of blood to his cock, stimulating an immediate erection. Beads of sweat formed on his forehead. People on both sides shifted uncomfortably.

His hand clamped down on her wrist. "We need to leave. Right now. There is not time to explain." He tugged her arm but she did not move.

Gwen snorted and rolled her eyes but made no effort to leave. "Why? I'm interested in hearing what he has to say."

Calder moved a few steps closer and Tyrel noticed. "Step off brother. You don't want a repeat of what happened last time."

"Nope, I don't," Calder snapped. "But if we don't get her out of here it may not matter."

Gwen was surprised by his words. She looked around, noticing that every man in the crowd was now looking her way. Every eye was locked on her, watching her every move. She suddenly had the urge to shift and run, not caring if Tyrel followed her. She took a step toward the trail head and Tyrel stopped her. Gwen's eyes locked with his and they spent almost a minute just staring eyes to eyes. When they finally broke contact and looked away, Ty's face was tight, his eyes dark. "It's too late. They know"

8

Chapter 24

Tyrel watched as Otto walked to the rock and spoke with Gideon. Gideon shook his head no, but Otto kept talking. His eyes never left Gwen. There was some type of argument, then Gideon's shoulders fell and he nodded.

"Attention. There has been a challenge issued for the right to mate with my daughter Gwen. Under Pride law, she is not a protected member as the binding ceremony has not taken place. Anyone interesting in answering the challenge please step forward. Would someone please escort Gwen to the Rock."

Gideon hated the distraught expression on Tyrel's face but had no choice in the matter. No one had not expected this to happen so soon. It had to be the presence of all the alpha males in one area. The panicked look on Gwen's face brought out his protective instinct, and he cursed the dead man who had brought this on. He was in no condition to answer a challenge. He would not be able to dance with the other alpha males tonight. Because of his injury the challenge was not only for mating rights. The winner would also take his place as the Prides Alpha and leader. This is what Otto had been waiting for and everyone knew it. He wondered how Otto intended to answer a challenge when he could not shift? The only way to know was to ask him.

"Otto, you do realize that the challenge is fought in both human and cat form. No weapons are allowed."

"I can beat these losers with my bare hands. Hell, with one hand. But don't worry about me. When the time comes, I will meet the challenge."

Gideon was surprised. Otto could shift? Looking back, he could not remember Otto saying he couldn't change forms. Only that he didn't.

Officer Davidson had been staring at Otto the entire time he was talking to Gideon. There was something about the burly mountaineer that was strangely familiar. Brett was certain he had seen him somewhere before today, but he could not figure out where that was. As a bonded male, he was not interested in the mating challenge, but as an alpha, her heat was still affecting him. He turned to Carl. " I need to go and check something in the car. I will be right back."

Carl nodded, thinking this was Brett's way of avoiding an uncomfortable situation. Gwen was a beautiful woman but there was no way he was going to get involved in what could easily become a death match.

Spectators were shifting around the clearing, making room for all the contestants to come forward. The area before the rock was cleared, leaving a space about fifty square feet in which the battle would be held. Several men had already stepped forward, ignoring Otto as if he were not worth their attention. Tyrel looked at Calder and raised an eyebrow, silently asking if he was going to join. Calder shook his head no. Tyrel sighed and walked toward the flat rock.

Chapter 25

Rick followed Brett when the Denver officer headed back to the precinct SUV. His instinct told him the out of town detective was onto something, and that something might be more important than who won the challenge and became the new leader of the Wolf Mountain Pride. He found Brett ensconced in the back seat of the Trail Blazer, scanning through photos on his laptop.

"Find anything interesting," he asked.

Brett looked up. "That Otto guy. I'm sure I have seen his face somewhere. I have no idea where but I'm certain of it. I looked through all the mugshots. No luck. There's something about him that is driving me crazy."

"Glad to know I'm not losing it. I felt the same way about him when he walked over to talk to Gideon. I don't know what it is. Maybe he just has one of those faces?"

"No. Its more than that. He connected somehow."

"Aren't you going to go back and watch the challenge?"

"You go on ahead. I think I'm gonna stay here and continue to go through the files. Otto is connected to something, somewhere. I've seen his face in a file somewhere. There's a reason it's sticking in my mind.

"Well, I have never seen a challenge match. My curiosity is overwhelming any good sense I have left after joining the force. I'm heading back to watch. Call it to on the job training or something like that." Rick's eyes gleamed in the moonlight. Blue eyes.

Brett laughed. "Until you said that, I hadn't bothered to ask. You're human, aren't you?"

Rick grinned. "Yeah. My wife calls me her hidden addiction. I think she categories me along with Coca Cola and chocolate in her mind.

"You guys have it made here. I can imagine the reaction if anyone on the Denver PD found out that they had shifters on the force. First they would think someone had drugged them. Then that they were going insane. Finally they would swear we were demons or aliens and try to kill us."

The Pride has been a part of the Smokey Mountains for a long time. The Tsalagi has kept the secret for longer than this country has existed. After so many years of intermarriage, it would be hard to find anyone willing to let the story out. If you change your mind, I will be over by the flat rock." Rick headed back to the clearing.

Brett continued to scan through the photos on his laptop. Suddenly he stopped. "Gotcha! I knew

I'd seen that smug bastard somewhere before." He hit the print button on the screen and waited.

***

As Rick approached the clearing he could feel the change in the atmosphere. There was an undercurrent of excitement amongst the viewers. Everyone was alert and waiting for the challenge to begin. He could hear Gideon reading off a list of rules. One surprised him no weapons were allowed. He had a reasonably good view of the fight grounds, there was only a small portion that was out of his view. He was surprised to see that Gwen was standing on the rock next to Gideon. Having her that close to the contestants had to be agitating them. He watched as her expression shifted from horror to shock to mild interest and wondered what she was experiencing. Since he was human he sensed none of the pheromones her body was putting out. The only males that appeared calm were Tyrel and Otto, even some of the grey haired grandfathers were behaving like teenagers. The two men were calmly removing their clothing, stripping down and folding them carefully to prevent damaging them during the fight. The other contestants had already shed their clothing. Three had shifted into their cat form, and the anxious mountain lions were pacing back and forth in front of the rock. Gideon had finished speaking and was now standing next to Gwen.

The twin alphas from Tennessee exchanged glances with each other. There was no official start. One second they were checking the competition out, the next they had shifted and were each going for another cougars throat. Their attack was followed by almost all of the aspirants. Two of the big cats took the most obvious route, charging directly at Otto. This surprised him.

Without his clothes, Otto had turned out to be bigger and more muscular than anyone had suspected. Instead of fat rolls, his clothing had hidden an extremely large frame with well-defined muscles. Beneath multiple tattoos, a spiders web of scars showed where he had been injured in the past. He snatched one of the twin cougars out of the air, tossing him across the clearing. The second leapt for his throat. Otto managed to grab a handful of skin before his teeth reached his neck. He pulled the Cougar tight against his body, preventing him from raking his chest and stomach with his claws, and began to squeeze.

Alarms went off in Tyrel's head as he saw the big man grappling with the cougar. Otto was fast. He had never seen anyone snatch a leaping mountain lion out of the air before. He watched as the second cougar fought against the vise like grip and lost. Otto was bending the cat back over the edge of the big rock. There was a loud snap as his spine gave way and then Otto shifted his hands to the cougars neck and began to squeeze. In seconds it was over as Otto dropped the dead cat on the ground at his feet.

The twin's brother snarled and charged back into the clearing, ignoring Tyrel in his drive for revenge. He managed to sink his teeth into Ottos' right leg, tearing a strip of meat loose before breaking away and leaping for his back, fastening his fangs in the muscles of Otto's shoulder. Once he had a grip he began raking his back and shoulders with his rear claws. He dug his front claws into both shoulders, using them to stay attached as he ripped and tore into Otto's flesh. Otto continued to swing, landing blow after blow on the big cats chest and head. One of his blows struck him in the temple, causing him to lose consciousness. He fell to the ground. Otto turned and began kicking the injured cat in the face and chest. Blood flowed freely from his nose and mouth. He seemed to be having difficulty taking a breath. The sorely battered cougar issued a raw moan from deep within his chest, followed by a shallow cough and a rumbling gurgle before he dropped to his stomach and slinked away.

Otto watched him go without comment. He was bleeding from multiple deep gouges along his back and shoulders. Several of the rips in his stomach were bleeding freely. But he was still standing and had no intention of leaving the field. He waited impatiently as four men rushed in and recovered the seriously injured cougar. The disabled twin had not reverted to human form, so he was still alive. Whether he would recover from the serious spinal injury was unknown.

Otto's dark brown eyes scanned the field noting that Tyler had not shifted. Nor had any of the other mountain lions attempted to take him out. This could mean two things...they respected his claim to the girl or they were afraid of him, maybe both. Neither option affected Otto's plan of action. The only way Tyrel was leaving the challenge field was in a body bag.

Only one cougar remained standing of the three rogues who had been fighting each other. One, had taken an injury to his eye and stomach. He decided he had enough and slunk away to get medical attention. The second cat was lying unconscious in a pool of blood and the recovery team was trying to slide him on a stretcher. The paramedic was doing his best to push the mutilated mans' internal organs back into the open body cavity. It was going to be a race to see if they could get him to the clinic before he died.

The surviving cougar's golden eyes had dilated until only a narrow yellow band surrounded the oversized black pupil. His tail moved from side to side in quick, nervous jerks. Otto thought he had been introduced as Jackson, from the same Pride as Calder. He was bigger than normal lion, almost as big as Otto. Jackson had no intention of making the same mistakes the others had. He intended to wait until Otto was in dire straits or at least starting to show signs of exhaustion before making his next move. His gut had told him Tyrel was the dangerous one. Still, he had underestimated Otto once and had no intention of doing it again.

Jackson yowled, letting some of the frustration he was feeling out. It would be easier to make some kind of plan if her scent had not been driving him crazy. How Ty could keep himself so calm after mating with her and forming a bond he couldn't understand. Wait. A bond? He could sense it now. Tyrel was bonded with Gwen. How did he miss it? The only way the bond could be broken was if Ty were dead. Jackson had no intention of fighting his friend to the death. Instead of attacking, he turned his neck up to Tyrel and then he walked off the field.

Otto's smirk as he conceded and walked off the field was easily seen by all the witnesses. Gwen felt a shiver run up her spine as she watched his reaction. Her grandmother used to say someone was walking over your grave in the future. She wasn't so sure that was the reason, but there was something about Otto that made her hair stand on end. It wasn't his attitude. Tyrel could be a real prick at times. That didn't affect her the way Otto did. She felt the urge to run and hide every time she was near the big man. She was afraid for Tyrel. Now that she had openly embraced their love anyone could easily feel the bond between them. Otto had to know it was there. That meant he intended to kill Ty, not simply fight him to first blood.

Like sumo wrestlers of old, the two men circled the clearing, watching for an opening that would give them an advantage in the contest. It seemed like things changed in between blinks; open they were apart, close and open again, they were locked together. At first it was a raucous free for all. Blows rose and fell like pistons, fists slamming into flesh with relentless brutality. She had never expected this level of violence. The two men exchanged punches, pounding their fists into rapidly discoloring flesh, made slick with sweat and blood. As quickly as they moved together, they moved apart and then back together. This time, it was almost as if they took turns exchanging deliberate bare-knuckled blows. First one , then the other man would be ahead. They finally realized neither had an advantage in the hand to hand contest and separated.

Gwen released a soft murmur of protest as Gideon tried to move her away from the front of the flat rock. There was no way she was leaving without Tyrel. He was holding his own against the bigger man, but she could see he was tired. Bright red blood flowed down Ty's face from a laceration above his right eye. It was already swollen and would likely affect his vision on that side. Otto was missing a front tooth and the side of his mouth was torn and bleeding. His nose was slightly out of line, likely broken when Ty's head had smashed into the bigger man's face. Both men were gasping for breath, their chests rising and falling rapidly as they fought for air. It was clear neither man was willing to give an inch and all she could do was watch…and wait.

Tyrel winced as the scent of Gwen's rising heat wafted on the wind his way. Her presence made it harder to keep his sanity, while reminding him of exactly what he stood to lose. It was a powerful incentive. Otto had to be fighting the urge, too. He wondered what the burly old rogue planned to do next.

That's when Otto began to shift.

It was obvious within seconds that Otto was not a normal mountain lion. For one thing, his coat was not tawny brown with black highlights. His coat was dark, almost black, more like a jaguar or leopard. Instead of a solid color, his fur was striped, like a tigers. But he wasn't a tiger. He was a mountain lion, just not a normal one.

"What the hell is he?" Gideon asked aloud the question in everyone's mind.

Brett whistled. " I'll be damned. That's why we were having trouble identifying him. He's a Liger. Take a look at this photo. He was in the crowd at the murder site. In Colorado."

"A Liger?" Gideon had never heard of a Liger.

"A Chimera. First one I've ever seen outside a zoo. A cross between a lion and a tiger. Usually it happens when they are penned up together for a long time. Cougars are rarely held in captivity. One of his parents must have been a tiger, one that escaped from a circus or a zoo. It might have given up on finding a mate and taken up with a mountain lion out of loneliness."

"So what do we do? We can't arrest a damn Liger. What if he doesn't shift back?"

"We wait and hope Tyrel figures out a way to win this lopsided challenge."

***

Tyrel realized there was a stone-faced killer standing across from him.. The fire of tightly restrained hate smoldered beneath his heavy brow. If looks could kill like the old saying goes, Gwen would already belong to Otto. He watched in awe as Otto began to shift into his cat form. Once again the big man had been caught in a lie. The shift might have been causing him pain, but he was able to complete the morph with no problem. Whatever Otto was; it was readily apparent he was not a cougar. Not with that size and coloring. He also had a good fifty pounds on him. Ty hoped he was faster, since he was going to need every advantage he could find. Otto was moving more like a bear than a big cat. But if he got those oversized claws into him, it was going hurt like a mutha pulling loose. He wasn't worried about shifting, he was worried about Otto sinking his teeth into his throat before he completed the morph.

Chapter 27

Rick kept his eyes locked on the two big cats circling the clearing, wondering which one would break first. It was hard to describe the speed of a charging lion. Otto was growling, and pacing his rage apparent in the sharp, whiplike motion of his sinuous tail. The oddly patterned animal raised his massive head and a low growl vibrated deep in his throat. As he paced, Otto's heavy jowls dripped saliva as he opened his mouth in a ferocious roar, showing off razor sharp teeth. He continued to shift his weight uneasily, drawing his hind quarters far beneath his tawny body, while gathering himself for a sudden charge. Deep brown eyes shot hungry fire. His great muscles quivered as the excitement of the moment built to a frenzy.

Tyrel had been watching carefully for any type of body signals. As they paced he noticed that Otto's eyes kept turning constantly toward the firelight. That was a bad decision. It would take his vision a few seconds to readjust once he turned away. That might give him a slight advantage during the initial attack. He tensed Otto's tail, which had been sweeping back and forth behind him, suddenly went erect, straight and stiff and sure sign of imminent attack.

Tyrel wasted no time wondering about the other cats intent. He began shifting as he ran, covering the distance between them in great leaps. Hurtling through the air, he met the liger in midleap, and managed to rip a gash in the bigger cats shoulder. As he passed, the charging liger's extended talons grazed him, scratching a bloody streak beneath along one hind quarter but doing no serious damage.

***

At the first sight of blood, Gwen sprang to her feet, her amber eyes blazing, arms crossed tightly beneath her breasts and watched as Tyrel moved his position. Half blinded by tears Gwen watched at the two big cats met in a furious storm of claws and fangs.

Rick moved too close to where she was standing, startling her. Without concern for her clothing, she shifted, then warned him away with a low growl. Seconds later, the female cougar stood alone at the edge of the flat rock. Raising her muzzle, she sniffed the air for imminent danger. With everyone's eyes on the fight, she knew she was a prime target if Otto had set up another kidnapping attempt. Gideon was sitting nearby, but while he was out of the wheelchair, he would not be able to protect her. She relaxed a bit when she saw Morgan standing next to the rock

When Anola lay down beside her, she turned her attention back to the fight.

***

The speed of the strikes and intensity of the battle made it difficult to tell Tyrel's tawny brown body from Otto's almost black one. The Liger had an obvious advantage in weight, yet the younger , more agile Cougar always managed to elude him with insolent ease. They broke apart, circled and then charged back together, biting and clawing at any available surface.

The bigger cat rose erect upon its hind legs, driving his claws deep into Ty's shoulder and back, the razor sharp edges gouging deep furrows into his straining muscles. Tyrel could not contain a roar of agony. Somehow the younger, lithe cougar twisted his body away; the sinewy movement preventing Otto from getting a secure grip. The pain was mind numbing; but as the talons relaxed their hold he realized they had not cut deep into the muscle.

To anyone watching the writhing, snarling knot of fighting beasts it was clear that neither cat was holding back. First blood had not slowed them in any way. The coats of both animals was mottled crimson from multiple bites and gashes. Otto had a wicked gash down the right side of his face, where Tyrel's talon cut him from the ear to his nose. His right eye was swollen and bloody; the curved claw may have blinded him permanently on that side.

Tyrel was in worse shape. Bitten and mangled, tearing and torn, Tyrel battled for his life against the much larger cat. The longer the fight continued, the greater the odds were against his survival. Otto's talons had left deep furrows on both shoulders, his back and head showed multiple bite marks, and he was dragging the same leg he had injured in the helicopter crash. It was going to come down to which was still on their feet when the other fell.

To the observers, Otto appeared to be slowing, his attacks becoming much easier for Tyrel to avoid.

To Ty, he was moving like an old lion whose failing strength and agility had forced him to live off any prey that he could catch. Cunning took the place of raw power. He dodged right, using Otto's diminished vision against him. Clawing desperately for traction in the soft dirt, he succeeded in out maneuvering his larger opponent. He leaped toward Otto's blind side, latched onto his shoulder and rolled his body, pulling Otto over onto the ground. Raising up upon his haunches, Ty's powerful back legs dug in, shredding the soft tissue of Otto's underbelly. He continued to kick until the smokey grey fur was tinged pink from the blood. The darker Liger managed to get in a paw thrust that ripped Tyrel's flank open, exposing the bone on his bad leg. The terrible wound shook the younger fighter and he roared as the wave of pain washed over him.

Gwen roared back her encouragement. From where she was sitting it looked like he was losing quite a lot of blood from the savage assault. Tyrel was much faster than the older man but Otto fought with the coolness and confidence of a veteran combatant. Both were gravely injured.

The two fighters separated and drew apart only to rush at one another again. Over and over they rolled, grappling and tearing; first the golden brown tail would whisk up in sight, then the black one. There was a flurry of teeth and talons. Then it slowed and everyone could see that Tyrel had his long fighting fangs buried up to the bone in the soft white fur of Otto's throat. Otto made a valiant effort but Ty's hold was too strong and his strength was too far gone.

From deep inside his chest the Tyrel issued a low rumbling roar that set stiff hairs to bristling throughout the watching crowd There was no mercy remaining in the golden ringed eyes. He continued to apply pressure until the light faded from the liger's eyes and he dropped unconscious to the ground.

Like it or not, he was now the Prides Alpha. Resigned to his new future, he began to morph back into human form. He stood over Otto's body, bright red streaking his face, his muscles rolling, and skin stained dark with his enemies blood. In a gesture of disgust, he drew the back of his forearm and hand across his mouth and then he wiped his bloody fingers upon Otto's fur. This was not what he wanted. The fight for supremacy had not been necessary. Gwen. He needed to get to Gwen.

He took a step and wavered, unsure if his leg would hold his weight. Several people rushed to help him walk. He brushed them away and hobbled to the rock on his own. As soon as the transformation was complete most of his wounds had closed. He felt steadier, but not ready for any further challenges. None came.

All he could think of was reaching his mate. She ran into his arms. That's when he realized he was no longer being influenced by her heat.

He raised one eyebrow and ran his fingers through his thick, black shock of hair; a habit Gwen had already learned meant he was puzzled. She laughed, "I guess the timing was perfect this morning."

"We can discuss it when we get home. Wait here. I need to talk to a few people before we leave." He limped over to where Morgan stood talking to a small group of councilmen.

Rick and the two Colorado officers made their way over to Otto's body, which was still in cougar form.

Brett let out a sharp whistle. " Damn, it's hard to believe he is still alive."

Rick laughed. "Shifters are hard to kill. But at least this way, you can take him back to stand trial."

"True. He still needs to be cuffed. The wounds will heal." As though he had heard their words, Otto's body blurred and he shifted back to human form.

The defeated challenger looked around, as if he were still puzzled by what had just happened before trying to rise to his feet. Once he was standing, he remained still, trying to regain his balance. Instead of walking away, and acknowledging his defeat, he looked around, spotting Ty talking to Gideon. Before Rick or Brett could react, he began running.

"Ty, watch out!" Rick yelled as he ran.

Then he realized Ty wasn't Ottos target. The big Ligers oversized hands clamped down on Gwen's wrist. Before she had a chance to pull away, he had tossed her over one shoulder and was stumbling toward the parking lot. She struggled to get away, but even injured, Otto was much stronger than she was.

"Someone help me," she screamed as she squirmed and beat on Otto's back. He ignored her and kept walking toward the trail from the clearing.

Gwen's panic stricken voice broke through the noise of congratulations. From the corner of his eye Tyrel spotted Otto carrying away his mate. All sense of protocol left his mind. His mate was in danger. He had already taken one child; he would not get a chance to hurt another. Tyrel ran toward the big man and with a prodigious leap, tackled him , bring them both to the ground once more. They rolled down the steep bank toward the rim of the creek. The landing had been sufficient to knock the breath out of Otto and free Gwen. To make sure he stayed down this time, Tyrel hit him three times. The hybrid shifter slid unconscious to the ground at his feet.

All three officers swarmed over him. Rick snapped a set of cuffs on Otto's wrists and Brett chained his feet. Then they dumped some creek water over him to wake him up.

No one remaining in the clearing asked why he was being taken away in chains. Billy and Pete had disappeared when Tyrel won the challenge. Rick would find them later. They had a few questions to answer.

Tyrel held Gwen until she stopped shaking. "Let's go home. We can let the family know later. They are going to be excited about the twins."

Twins? "Ty! What twins? Wait a minute. Stop walking. You're ignoring me. Why did you mention twins? ...Ty! Answer me damn it. What twins. Ty!"